MEASURED DECEPTION

A NICK BLAINE MYSTERY

RICHARD E. KALK
T. ANN PRYOR

BASED ON A TRUE STORY

To our families who believed in our crazy idea

And for Uncle Richard who lived it

PROLOGUE

Dear Little Brother;

At your command, I am enclosing your ticket to come out to Los Angeles. Ainsley, I would prefer for me to come there and see you and you stay there in Chicago. I won't be able to watch over you here because I got a robbery case going in New Orleans. I will have to make several trips down there on this case. Don't worry. I'll be alright. This is a five-million-dollar gold shipment robbery in the making and I'm assigned to it.

I do miss you very much and I am just thanking God that you are all alright after that attack. We're lucky that maniac didn't kill you. I wish you had told me you were walking over to my house that night. I've always told you, never walk the streets alone or be out there by yourself. I could seek revenge on the bastard(s) that hurt you, but, an eye for an eye leaves us all blind and there is no justice. But, rest assured, whoever it was won't have any luck down the way. In the meantime, stop telling your friends what I give you. They're not who they say they are.

I'm going to talk to your mom about you coming to L.A. I would pay for you to go to beauty school there in Chicago if you would stay put. California is too fast for you. Yes, I know I that I will be without you if you're there, but I can always come and see you and still take care of you as I always have done. I want you to finish beauty school so bad, and you can have a shop at your house and make lots of money.

I am sending you some cash, but please slow down on your spending. I will call you from New Orleans later this week when or when I get there. Don't worry about me. I can take care of myself. Just don't let any of your so-called friends know what type of work I do. They might feel comfortable breaking the law and expecting me to get them out of a jam.

I got to run to get this letter in the mail. When you get it, call and give me a code so I will know you got the ticket and the money. I'm going to get you some Blue Cross or Blue Shield there, so if you ever need to go to a doctor or get sick, you won't have to go to the

County hospital. Although, you probably won't ever get sick because you don't let nothing worry you. Sign up for the Blue Cross and let me know what the payments are, and I will take care of it.

I don't see any of those boys that used to come around when you were here. I guess they got the message that I don't mess around and they don't need to call or come by. All of them knew you were gone, and they were still calling and trying to get next to me.

You will have to excuse this letter. I'm in a hurry to get it in the mail. How are your mom and little Jimmy? Give my regards to all of your family for me. If I get the job in New Orleans, I'll take you there with me, but I really don't want you coming back to Los Angeles. Try and get your credits done there in Chicago. If it takes more money, I will just have pay for it.

Say, you left the t.v. in the car, you forgot to take it. I will keep it in memory of you. Okay, I can send the t.v. to you or bring it when I come see you. You take care and keep in touch and please stay in church. I love you, very much.

Love,

Rodney

1

January 1984

Conrad Knowles was feeling good. Caught up in that state of alcohol infusion that straddles euphoria and melancholy, he was leaning toward the former. An older man caught his eye across the dance floor, and they were sizing up one another when Ainsley Brown sidled up to the bar, dripping with sweat and nervous energy.

"Hey," he yelled over the music to Conrad. "We need to go. It's nearly two."

"So?" Conrad replied while gazing at the men across the way.

"I need to be back in case Rodney calls."

"I just got a fresh drink and am thinking of making a new friend." Conrad gestured toward his quarry.

"Oh hell," Ainsley wailed. "That's Carl. Everybody here has slept with Carl."

"I haven't."

"Let's move. You know how Rodney is if I'm out all night."

Rodney Williams. Conrad could barely contain his contempt and fear of the man. Just hearing the name caused instinctive eye-rolling. "Man, you need to cut that guy off." He took a large gulp of his drink.

"Now that I'm done with school, I can," Ainsley assured him. "But not tonight, so let's go."

Conrad downed his vodka tonic and made a final passing glance at Carl before letting Ainsley take him by the elbow and guide him out the door to the car Rodney had lent them. It was useless to argue with Ainsley about his benefactor, but Conrad was just drunk enough to try. "Man, you have to tell Rodney you're not his mistress."

"You know it's not like that."

"Isn't it? The man showers you with money and presents, and you do whatever he tells you."

"It's not like that," Ainsley argued. "He's just looking out for my mom and us."

Conrad had heard that line before. "So, he's looking out for your well-being?"

"Yeah, I guess so."

"And he's looking after you for your mama?"

"Yes."

"Well, did he tell your mama that someone attacked and tried to kill your ass right after you got to Los Angeles?"

"Don't be stupid," Ainsley was getting irritated.

"Has Rodney told her how much he's into you?"

" You know it's not like that with Rodney. And you know that my mom doesn't know about the men in my life. She has no idea I'm gay."

"Doesn't she?" Conrad was incredulous that Coretta Brown had no idea her older son was homosexual. He had never gone to any lengths to pretend otherwise.

"Look," Ainsley said as he pulled over to the curb in front of the building where they were staying, "We're on that plane tomorrow, and when we get back to Chicago, I'll call Rodney and have a talk with him about backing off."

"Sure, sure." Conrad derided.

"Shhh... who is that?" Ainsley asked as he looked out the windshield.

A man came around the building and out of the

shadows onto Normandie Avenue, where they were parked. He stood in front of the vehicle and pulled something from his pocket. It appeared to be a small piece of paper. He quietly stared at it a moment before looking at Conrad and Ainsley and back again.

Ainsley rolled down the window to holler at the man and find out his business. He didn't have time to react to the gunshots fired into the car.

PANCHO VILLA'S, a little restaurant not far from LAPD's Rampart Division, was relatively quiet in the late afternoon. The cops who frequented at lunch and after shift had either already left or were yet to come. Still, Martha was mixing a batch of her famous margaritas while her husband, Manuel, tended to the grill.

In a large, red booth tucked away in the farthest corner of the place, a reporter sat, listening with rapt attention as he was regaled by a middle-aged policeman of days and crimes long gone by.

Lawson Daly had worked for the paper for several years and never tired of meeting up with a member of the police force. Their tales were fascinating—especially those of Detective Sergeant Nick Blaine.

Blaine's long-time partner, John Phillips, once described the man as having a face like a catcher's mitt. Daly wasn't sure that was an accurate portrayal. It was true that Blaine was pushing fifty and a little round in the midsection, but he was tall and sturdily built. He had lost his hair ages ago, as well as his 20/20 vision. Yet, he had a youthful, virile, quality.

Daly couldn't help but notice that Blaine looked like a man who knew what a hard day at work was like. He admired that about him as he sat in the booth, sipping his beer and listening as Blaine explained why he had been awarded the LAPD's prestigious Medal of Valor.

"I was in plain clothes, and it was pouring rain, so I wore an overcoat. The guy had no idea I was a cop. My former partner, Detective George Romero, didn't want to get wet, so he waited in the car while I ran quickly to deposit my check. I went in the back door but noticed this guy come in from the other direction. Something wasn't right about him."

"You could tell that by looking at him?" Daly asked between bites of chili verde.

"Maybe not by looking at him. It was more of a gut feeling."

"Ah," Daly said through a mouthful of food, "The ol' cop's gut."

Blaine smiled knowingly as he continued. "The teller helping me walked away from the window for a brief moment, and I noticed out of the corner of my eye that same guy was at the window next to me. He took a brown bag out of his coat and handed it to the teller, and then pulled that coat back a bit and tapped on the handle of what looked like a .38 tucked into the waistband of his jeans."

Daly chewed slowly. His attention was focused on Blaine's story.

Blaine took a sip of his beer. "I was tense and aware there were people at the bus stop directly in front of the building. It was a congregation of potential victims out there if that jerk started shooting up the place. I tried to think of ways I could minimize the casualties.

"The teller came back, and I tried to catch her attention by saying she made a mistake. I thought she would go to the back again to figure out what she had done wrong, and that would get her out of danger. But she hesitated and looked at me funny before insisting the numbers were right and tried again to hand me the paper.

"'To better assess the situation, I turned as though I was leaving. But the guy was on to me. He flashed the butt of that revolver and told me, 'Be cool.'"

"What did you do?" Daly asked, nearly breathless with anticipation.

"Well," Blaine went on, "The man motioned for the teller at his window to clean out her cash drawer and the drawer of the teller who had been helping me. Luckily, it wasn't her first rodeo either, and before turning over the cash, she triggered the silent alarm.

"As she handed him the bag of cash, I relied on my old high school wrestling moves. I jumped behind him to secure his hands and bounce him. But the sucker was quick and got his left arm free. He used it to grab a display that had been on the counter and hit me over the head with it."

"Did it hurt?"

"It was cardboard. He tried to run for the door, but I had a grip on his right wrist. I seized his shoulder in a badly conceived attempt to wrangle him to the floor.

"Now, I'm not a young man, and I wasn't then either. I was forty-one, and this was some young guy who was in much better shape than me. So, we dragged each other around quite a bit as he tried to get free, and I tried to stop him. I finally got him on the floor and was able to get him on his belly."

"And then?"

"I was exhausted, so I laid down on top of him to

keep him still and catch my breath. I asked one of the tellers to go round back and get Romero.

"Later I learned she ran out into the downpour, tapped on the window, and told him I needed him inside. Romero told her to bugger off, that I was fine. He wasn't going out in the rain. She kept at him, though, and finally got him to roll down the window. She told him I was pinning down a would-be bank robber and needed backup. Well, that, of course, got him moving, and he rushed in. When he saw me sprawled out on top of the guy, he made some smart-ass remark like, "You told me you were depositing a check, not getting in your cardio for the month.""

Daly was amused. Blaine was a fascinating subject for his story. He had tried to interview Blaine's old partner, the famous crime writer Justice Steele. But Justice didn't have time and suggested Nick Blaine in his stead. Daly was finding it to have been a fair trade. Not only was he getting a night of good food and great entertainment, but he was gaining insight into one of the more celebrated officers in the LAPD.

"So, Sergeant," Daly said between bites of tortilla chips, "When you're not on the job, what do you and the wife like to do?"

Blaine grew quiet. "We haven't done anything for a long time," he replied. "Helen passed a few years ago."

Daly apologized. Steele hadn't relayed that information.

Blaine's countenance grew wistful as he recalled the family he used to have.

Daly hardly knew Blaine, but felt there was more than heartache in the officer's voice. Regret maybe? He looked up from his beer and noticed that Blaine's mind was far away and his eyes bleary, but just for a moment.

Blaine quickly composed himself before saying, "Did Steele ever tell you about the '68 riots?" He leaned back in his seat and began to regale Daly with exploits from twenty years prior as he and the reporter continued to drink and swap stories.

As they talked, they were joined by other off-duty officers meandering in for a quick one before going home, keeping Martha's blender whirring well into the night.

2

The remnants of the previous night's margaritas exacerbated the blare of the ringing phone on the nightstand as it reverberated in Blaine's skull. Thrashing his hand about blindly in the dark of the early morning, he finally found the receiver and pulled it to his mouth. "Hello?" He barked at the caller.

"Sergeant?" the clerk asked timidly.

"I think so," Blaine replied.

"There's been a murder." The voice continued to relay the pertinent information while Blaine picked up the glass of water from the nightstand and began gulping to thwart his oncoming hangover. He did not hear much of what was being said but knew Phillips would have all the details when he arrived.

Blaine hung up and made his way to the bathroom, splashed cold water on his face, and fuzzily gazed into the mirror. His pale blue eyes were bloodshot, but the rest of him didn't look too worse for wear. He smoothed down the few hairs that still clung in a ring around his balding head and quickly brushed his teeth before going into the closet to dig for clean clothes.

Clean clothes were never a problem when his wife was alive. Now, he had to remind himself to do laundry, usually after failing to find a clean pair of socks. Just as he felt as though he was getting himself back together, the wrinkle in his suit jacket brought on that sense of defeat and mourning. Sitting on the bed to put on his shoes, he looked up and saw the sticky note on the dresser with "do laundry" scrawled on it.

After pouring himself into his least rumpled suit, Blaine ambled into the kitchen to slug back a cup of the blackest coffee his old Mr. Coffee machine could expel. It was bitter but doing the job of waking him.

HE WAS SITTING QUIETLY, his head resting between his hands, waiting for the brew to do its job and reminding himself that he was too old to drink as he had the night before when he heard the front door open, followed by the familiar footsteps of his partner coming down the hall and into the kitchen.

Long and tan, Detective John Phillips was a good-looking man. His cheeks were high, and his jawline was chiseled. His luxurious, dark brown hair matched his eyes, and his thick, equally dark mustache covered his lip just enough to conceal the sneaky grin that often punctuated his mouth.

"You know, if you don't lock your doors at night, any creep off the street can waltz in," he said as he poured himself a cup of black sludge from the coffee pot.

"Yeah," Blaine returned. "One just did."

"You look like hell,"

"If you're going to be that way, we'll postpone the wedding until I get a facelift."

"Forget it. My parents wouldn't approve. You're too old for me."

"Like you could do better."

The two made their way out to their unmarked, department-issued Ford. It was the size of a small yacht and lacked all of the amenities of a rowboat.

"Do you know anything about what we've got?" Blaine asked as Phillips steered their boat through the city.

"One dead and one injured."

"Anyone we know? Blaine asked, referring to the killer.

That summer, Los Angeles was plagued with a number of boogeymen on the loose, and each came with a media-conceived moniker meant to terrorize the city further. The Grim Sleeper, Hillside Strangler, and Night Stalker led the headlines.

"I hope not," Phillips replied. "So far, though, nobody has mentioned any calling cards."

ARRIVING AT THE SCENE, Blaine noted how little light there seemed to be on the street. He wasn't surprised. Most of the street lamps were broken, much like the citizens of the surrounding area. He doubted the wonky street lamps were the only problem the denizens of the area had to put up with. "What's the story?" he asked a patrolman hovering nearby.

"Two men, both in their mid-twenties. The victim here is Ainsley Brown. His friend, Conrad Knowles, was taken in a bus to the hospital right before you got here. The two have been staying here at the Barclay." The younger officer gestured toward the rundown dwelling to their right. "Knowles said they got in around 2 a.m., but before they got out of the car, some guy started firing at them. Both were shot inside the vehicle. Brown perished on the scene. The crime lab has been called, but they said they're having a busy night and will get here when they get here."

"Any witnesses?" Blaine asked as he knelt and pulled the sheet back off the victim.

"At least ten, but nobody that saw anything."

"Sounds right."

The young man on the ground looked barely old enough to drive, Blaine thought as he wondered what the kid's story was. Everyone had a story. The city preyed upon the ambitions of those seeking to transform themselves. Was this kid in L.A. to chase the footlights of fame as so many others had before him? Or did his prorations lay somewhere outside the public realm? Perhaps he had wanted to be a doctor or, heaven forbid, a lawyer. The city was filled with opportunities. One just had to stay alive long enough to take advantage of them.

Blaine and Phillips spoke with other patrolmen and possible witnesses in the area while waiting for the coroner's man to arrive. Two hours later, she finally did.

"Detectives," the crime tech acknowledged as she strode up confidently.

"Not in a hurry, I see," Phillips said half-jokingly.

"I go in the order they send me. Given how over-worked and short-staffed we are, they send me every-where." She set the bag down and extended her hand. "Cynthia Liu," she said by way of introduction.

"Detective Phillips," Blaine replied, bending his head toward his partner, "and I'm Sergeant Detective Blaine."

"Blaine," she echoed, "I've heard of you."

"All bad, I imagine."

"Would you want it otherwise?"

Phillips rolled his eyes and groaned a little before inquiring if the tech would like to see the body. He noted the severity of the bun into which she had pulled back her jet-black hair as well as the large glasses she wore over her cobalt eyes. He thought she was going out of her way to disguise her attractiveness. Given her laser focus on the crime scene, Phillips wondered whether Blaine even noticed Cynthia Liu was a woman. Aptly enough, Cynthia Liu's gender was not lost on Phillips.

"Looks like the young man was shot with a .22 caliber," Cynthia observed. "The bullet entered here on the left side of his chest, and..." She rolled the body onto its side and looked under the collar of his shirt, "It got stuck here between his flesh and the fabric of his shirt. There's a second bullet hole here in his clavicle, but it doesn't appear to be through and through like this first one. I'll know more once we get him downtown. In the meantime, here's his wallet." Liu's gloved hand reached into the young man's front pocket, pulled out an old, worn, leather pouch, and handed it to Blaine, who had a quick rifle through it.

"What do we have?" Phillips asked.

"He's from Chicago," Blaine said as he tossed the wallet to Phillips.

"He's got quite a bit of money in here," Phillips observed. "A couple hundred dollar bills. That's a lot to be carrying around. Especially this close to Skid Row."

Blaine turned and motioned for Officer Ramirez, the first cop on the scene, to join them.

"Ramirez," Blaine acknowledged. "Where was the body when you arrived on scene?"

"He was in the car, sir."

"Who moved him?"

"I did, sir. I wasn't sure if he was still alive. His head was leaning on the window, so when I opened the door to check for a pulse, he started to slide out toward me. I grabbed him and pulled him out onto the street in case CPR was necessary to revive him."

"And?"

"He was gone, sir. No pulse, no sign of life."

"Phillips," Blaine gestured.

Reading his partner's mind, Phillips stepped over and began a preliminary search of the car, careful not to get blood on his bespoke suit.

"The car is registered to a Rodney Williams," Phillips advised his partner while searching the glove compartment.

"I've heard that name before," Blaine thought aloud. "Recently. No idea where, though."

"Yeah, it seems familiar to me, too," Phillips agreed as he continued to poke around the vehicle. "There's not a lot of blood on the passenger side," he noted.

"The other victim, Conrad Knowles, was shot in the arm," Ramirez interjected.

"And Brown on the left side of his body," Liu interjected.

"The shooter must have come up to the driver-side window and shot from there," Blaine noted as he stood up and surveyed the scene.

"That would explain why the windshield is intact," Phillips concurred.

"Anything else?" Blaine inquired of Cynthia Liu.

"Yes, based on the size of the wounds, your victim was shot up close and personal. The killer was a few feet away when he fired."

Liu then motioned for the man standing near her van to prepare the body for departure.

Blaine nodded and started to ponder what happened to Ainsley Brown. He looked up and scanned the small crowd gathered on the opposite side of the street. He didn't know if they were acquainted with the dead man or if they were just gawkers, morbidly fascinated by the murder in their community.

The Sergeant was unaware that among the onlookers stood the killer, watching with an intense curiosity, sizing up the detectives, and finding Blaine to have the potential to be a worthy adversary.

3

Conrad Knowles was visibly shaken as he recounted what had happened to him and his friend Ainsley early that morning. He kept going over their last few hours together. He remembered watching Ainsley on the dance floor of the club and wondered if the detective standing nearby could sense his jealousy.

"Mr. Knowles?" the detective inquired.

Startled from his reverie, Conrad attempted to sit up, but the searing pain in his arm took hold of him, and for a moment, all he could concentrate on was the bullet hole in his arm. He had never known this level of agony and wondered if a shot in the arm created this much anguish. How did people get through being shot anywhere else? Solemnly, he reminded himself that Ainsley didn't.

Conrad realized that Blaine had asked him a question. Tears stained his cheeks as he sat in the hospital bed and relived the trauma he experienced in the early morning hours. "We were parking the car outside of the place we were staying, and this guy—he came from the side of the building and walked toward us. He just walked up to the car like he was going to say something. At first, it seemed almost like he knew us and had been waiting for us to get there. Then, he stopped walking and kinda looked at us through the windshield. He was holding something, like a small piece of paper. He kept looking at whatever was in his hand and back at us. Then he stepped to the side of the car and started firing at us through Ainsley's open window."

Blaine sat in the acute sterility of the medical center. It was clear Conrad was nervous. His eyes darted everywhere as he spoke, and his hands shook with the violent anxiety of someone who felt like prey. He was going to blow town as soon as he got the chance. Of this, Blaine was certain.

"What did the man look like, Conrad?" Blaine tried to refocus his witness. He needed to get as much information as possible before Conrad flew the coop.

"I don't know. He was dark like me. Dark hair, dark skin. But the street lamps were dim. He coulda been anyone."

"What else?" the cop pressed for more.

"I don't know. He started shooting at us."

"Was he tall? Short? Was he old? Young?

Conrad tried to focus. "I don't know. Maybe as tall as me? I don't know how old. I couldn't see his face. He was there and looking down, and then all I could see was the flash from the gun. I think he shot me first and then Ainsley. There was no time to get out of the car. We had no idea he was going to fire on us. We were going back to Chicago today." Conrad whispered the last part, his eyes cast down as the weight of the night pressed on him.

"Walk me through your night, Conrad," Blaine encouraged.

He let out a deep sigh. "Ainsley had graduated earlier in the day from beauty school. That's why I'm here. I came out from Chicago for the graduation. We had gone to the graduation: Ainsley, Rodney, and me. Then we went and had dinner."

"Who is Rodney?"

"Rodney Williams. I don't know him very well. He said he was Ainsley's godfather, but I don't think that's true. All I know is that Rodney knows Ainsley's mom and family back in Chicago. He's known them for years, and sometimes he calls Ainsley his brother, sometimes his son, and sometimes his godson. He goes to see them all the time back there, and he sends them money."

Conrad paused a moment to wipe his face with the tissue Blaine handed him before continuing. His eyes were sorrowful, the dimples in his cheeks turned downward as though they would never know how to smile again. "Rodney has been sending money to Ainsley and his mom for I don't know how long. I just know that he was giving 'em money. Rodney told Ainsley he would help him pay for beauty school and to get started with his own shop in Chicago after graduation."

"A beauty parlor in Chicago and not here in Los Angeles?"

"Yeah. Rodney kept telling Ainsley that L.A. wasn't safe for us."

Blaine was intrigued. "Unsafe for you? Why?"

Conrad peered down with embarrassment while Blaine reflected on Ainsley's clothes and the reputation of the bar Conrad had mentioned they had been at the night before.

Blaine nodded to Conrad and spoke softly, "It's okay."

Both men took a deep breath and looked at each other to acknowledge what was unsaid between them. It wasn't something most people spoke about. Blaine didn't care much what other people wanted to do with their lives. They were their lives. But Conrad obviously didn't want to talk about it.

"So," Blaine continued after several moments pause. "Do you think Rodney was concerned for Ainsley based on his lifestyle?"

"I don't know," Conrad admitted. "I would have bet you Rodney himself was gay, but then when he got angry at Ainsley, he would scream at him and call him terrible names."

"Such as?"

"Faggot, for one," Conrad replied. "Then, on other occasions Rodney was all over Ainsley with phone calls and demands for his time. I thought maybe they had something going on, but Ainsley swore they didn't."

"Oh?" Blaine remarked before realizing he had sounded surprised.

"You thought Ainsley and I were together?" Conrad queried.

Blaine nodded.

"We used to be. Once in a while, we would hook up, but usually, it was when Ainsley was bored or between relationships. His relationships didn't last very long."

"Hmm," Blaine thought, "Phillips should understand that." He tried to recall his partner's longest relationship in the dozen or so years they had known each other. Six months, maybe? He started to wonder how long it would be before Phillips made a go at Cynthia Liu before he realized his mind was wandering and quickly turned back to Conrad. "Okay, so Ainsley graduated, and then what happened last night?"

"We went to dinner. Rodney took us out to celebrate. I don't know the name of the place. I don't know Los Angeles very well. This is my first time here. After dinner, we were going to go to the movies and then to a club, but Rodney changed his mind at the last minute and said he didn't want to go. He asked us to take him home."

"Did Rodney mention why he didn't want to go to the movies?"

Conrad sighed. "I don't think he's comfortable going out in public with Ainsley and me. I think Ainsley was too comfortable in his own skin for Rodney's liking. Ainsley on his own, maybe that was okay, but Ainsley told me that whenever he had a friend with him, Rodney could get unpredictable."

"Okay," Blaine said before pressing Conrad to continue.

"So, we took Rodney home. Then, he started acting kinda squirrelly."

"Squirrelly, how?"

"Like, he wanted all this information from us. He asked us where we were going. Ainsley told him we were gonna go to Trini's in Silverlake. Rodney told us to be careful. He talked on and on about some serial killer going after gay men all the time, but we haven't heard anything about that from no one but Rodney. Then he asked us when we would be going home, and Ainsley told him he didn't know, but it would be late, maybe around two a.m. Rodney said okay and then did something really strange. Or at least I thought it was strange."

"What did he do?"

"He asked each of us for a picture of ourselves. I didn't have one and wasn't gonna give him one anyway, but Ainsley gave him one he had in his wallet of him with his mom."

"Do you know what Rodney was going to do with the pictures," Blaine inquired.

"No idea. He already had pictures of Ainsley. One is framed in his living room on a table."

"Okay, go on."

"After that, Rodney wanted to know again where we were going and when we would be back home. Ainsley told him a second time we would probably go dancing at the club and be back around two a.m. Rodney was always jealous. He acted like he didn't want Ainsley going out and meeting people, especially men. When Rodney visited Chicago, he would follow Ainsley when he went out. I was with him a couple of times. Rodney didn't even bother to hide. He would just follow plain as day."

"And Ainsley denied a relationship with Rodney?"

"Yeah, and Rodney would fly off the handle when anyone even implied he was gay. I first met him, I asked how long him and Ainsley had been together. He threatened to kill me. He grabbed my throat, pulled a gun out of his pants, and held it to my head. Told me if I ever called him a faggot again, he'd put a bullet in my head."

"Nice guy," Blaine observed wryly as he made note of Rodney's behaviors. "Please, go on."

"We wound up at Trini's like Ainsley had planned. I didn't know anyone there, but Ainsley—he knew everyone. He was like that, ya know? He liked everyone, and everyone loved him. Near the end of the night, Donna Summer was playing. I love her music..."

Conrad's voice trailed off as he slipped into the memory of the night before.

The clear ring of Donna Summer's voice permeated the tight spaces between the moving bodies on the club's dance floor. Conrad had been watching Ainsley from a stool at the bar. Conrad didn't dance, but he liked to watch Ainsley. Both men were enjoying the throws of youth, But Ainsley seemed to be enjoying it more than his friend.

Conrad assessed his friend and admitted to himself as he watched the other dancing that he was jealous of Ainsley's lithe frame, shrewd fashion taste, and beguiling demeanor. Conrad felt like a behemoth next to Ainsley, and on the dance floor, his feet were never sure of their purpose. Conrad's face often betrayed the bitterness he kept stifled deep within.

Ainsley had electrified the club and everyone around him. The most Conrad could hope for was to stay in Ainsley's orbit, but he knew it wouldn't last long and was saddened, knowing he had been right. Relationships with people like Ainsley rarely lasted long. The world fed on the flashing light of stars like Ainsley Brown. And so, Conrad watched his friend dance.

Blaine let Conrad revel in his thoughts for a moment, hoping it would produce something constructive for the investigation. Finally, as it seemed Conrad was becoming absorbed by his reflections, Blaine prompted the young man back to reality and asked him to continue.

"Oh. After the club, we went back home. Ainsley promised Rodney we'd be back around two a.m., and Ainsley hated to upset Rodney. We had just pulled up and were parking the car. That's when that guy came out and started shooting at us."

"At any time, did the man say anything to you?" Blaine queried.

Conrad winced when Blaine mentioned the shooting. He closed his eyes as tight as he could and touched his arm. The searing pain brought back that moment, but he didn't want to relive it. He wanted to bury it as deep as he could and leave it there.

"Mr. Knowles?" the detective beckoned.

Conrad kept his eyes closed, willing Blaine and the recollection of the night before to go away. But he knew Blaine wasn't going anywhere until he got what he wanted.

"No," Conrad slowly opened his eyes and peered at the cop. "He just looked at us, like I said. I don't know how to describe it. I don't know if I'm remembering it right. I just don't know." He was bewildered and alarmed but continued, "I swear it was almost like the guy was checking to make sure he had the right people."

Blaine wondered if the attack had been a hit and, if so, on whom. Ainsley or Conrad?

"Okay," Blaine said as he rose to depart. "I'd like you to stay in the area in case we need to speak with you again." Blaine knew that Conrad wasn't going to stay. He was pretty sure he already had a ticket home. But he handed the man his card, adding, "If you think of anything else, you call me."

Conrad nodded in compliance and watched as the detective left his room.

He was back in Chicago before the end of the day.

4

As they hunkered down in their favorite greasy spoon, Blaine found himself relishing the orchestral cacophony found only in a diner at midday. He took a big drink of his coffee, thankful the diner's was better than what he made at home. He could not yet fathom the idea of food. His stomach was still full of margaritas and regret. He knew he had reached an age where a hangover lasted forever, and he was on day one of what promised to be a week-long headache. As usual, he asked himself if it had been worth it. As usual, he wasn't exactly sure it hadn't been.

"Hey," Phillips said, snapping his fingers, "Are you listening to me?"

"No," Blaine replied honestly.

"Try. I was saying when I was at Ainsley's apartment, I met an interesting tenant while waiting for the landlord to arrive. Missy Endicott. She lived next door to Ainsley and knew him."

"Oh?" Blaine re-engaged in the conversation.

"Yeah, she said that a few nights ago the landlord, this guy Ronnie Hall, had been in Ainsley's apartment. She heard them screaming at each other."

"About what?"

"She couldn't hear it all, but she did make out that Hall wanted Ainsley out before the end of the week. But Ainsley reminded him that Rodney person had paid up until the end of the month."

"Did she know why Hall was tossing the kid?" Blaine inquired.

"Nope, she didn't catch that part. She found it funny, though, given that Hall spent so much time at Ainsley's apartment. According to her, there were always parties going on. She had been to a few herself when she wasn't working nights. She's a waitress over at Norm's on Sunset."

"Did she see what happened last night?"

"She was at work," Phillips answered.

"Too bad. So, what did Hall have to say for himself?"

"Well," Phillips continued, "When he finally

dragged himself to his office, he reeked of weed and liquor and looked like he had been hit by a truck."

"I know the feeling," Blaine rubbed his temples.

"I asked him where he was last night, and he said he was out with friends. First, they were at the Palisade, and then they went on to Sorento's, where they were until closing at five a.m. After that, he went to Norm's for breakfast and to see Missy. He said he got back around eight a.m. and passed out drunk."

"That's convenient," Blaine pondered aloud. "Do we know anything else about Hall?"

"Small-time crook with arrests for petty theft and some shoplifting."

"That's curious. How did a thief get to be a landlord?"

"I agree. How did it go down at the hospital?"

Blaine told Phillips about his meeting with Conrad before the two headed to the precinct.

BLAINE HAD BEEN at his desk for less than an hour, slowly sifting through the witness statements. Each narrative seemed strikingly like the one before it: the person didn't see or notice anything until they heard the gunshots. Several people queried claimed they didn't hear anything, while others admitted ignoring the noise and going back to sleep.

The building had known better days, glamorous ones. Just sixty years before, it was a hotel frequented by L.A.'s "it crowd."

It wasn't a shock to Blaine or Phillips that not a soul heard or saw anything. Many of the tenants worked hard and saved their money to move up in the world. Those who didn't were too high or stoned to care if someone had been killed.

"How's it going on your end?" Blaine queried Phillips

"The usual." Phillips sat across from Blaine. Statements of those who had seen and heard nothing littered his desk. He was startled out of his annoyance with the lack of testimony from Ainsley's neighbors by the shrill ring of the telephone sitting near his elbow on the edge of the desk.

"Phillips." The detective announced to the caller.

"Detective Phillips?" the voice on the other end asked quietly.

"It is. And this is?"

"I'm no one," a voice replied quietly after hesitating. "I have information about Ainsley Brown, but I'm not coming in, and I'm not testifying. He's too dangerous. I'm not getting myself killed."

Phillips snapped his fingers in the air, motioning to Blaine that the call was important. Blaine jumped up and came to his partner's desk, bending over to attempt to hear the voice on the other end. Phillips started to scribble notes as he asked, "Who is too dangerous?"

"I... I can't tell you that."

Phillips jotted onto a notepad that he thought the voice sounded like that of a female before he silently conveyed the caller's lack of participation to Blaine. They exchanged puzzled looks.

Blaine motioned for Phillips to keep the caller on the line. Maybe if they helped the person to relax, she might tell them who she was.

"That's okay," Phillips replied in a calm, smooth voice.

Blaine recognized it as one of the tools his partner employed when working on getting a phone number for a date. "Just take it one step at a time."

The woman seemed to gulp air as she tried to decide whether she should have called. An eternity later, she finally started to speak meekly. "There was a previous attempt to kill him," she relayed.

Phillips waited anxiously for her to reveal more, but after a long silence, he pressed for more information. "Who?" he asked.

"Ainsley Brown."

Surprised at the revelation, Phillips quickly asked, "Who tried to kill him?"

"I... I'm sorry. I shouldn't have called you." The line went dead.

Frustrated, Phillips jostled the phone's ringer for several seconds in a futile attempt to get the caller back on the line. Finally, he gave up. "What was that?" he asked

Blaine was still sitting on the edge of the desk.

"What could have that poor girl so scared she couldn't even speak?" Phillips wondered.

"Or who has her so scared?" Blaine countered. He wasn't sure, but knew he didn't like the feeling he had in the pit of his stomach. It was telling him this case was not going to be easy.

Under the glare of the fluorescent lights, Blaine and Phillips sat at opposite ends of Rampart Division's conference room table. A lumbering reticence hung over the room. The four visitors had arrived that morning, demanding to speak with the police officers in charge of the murder of Ainsley Brown. Now they sat, their faces etched with a mixture of grief and apprehension.

Phillips seemed to have been infected by the contagion of worry as his features betrayed a turmoil writhing within.

Blaine was curious as to what could be vexing his partner, but more pressing issues were at hand. "As I said in the lobby, I'm Sergeant Detective Blaine, and this is my partner, Detective Phillips.

"Detective, I want to know why my brother's killer hasn't been arrested yet."

Blaine turned to better assess the speaker, a diminutive woman with an ethereal quality further enhanced by her closely cropped hair and dark doe eyes.

"I'm sorry, I didn't get your name."

"Monica Brown. I'm Ainsley's older sister. Rodney Williams killed my brother. You need to arrest him."

Rodney Williams. That name kept coming up.

"What makes you think Rodney Williams murdered your brother?" He asked politely.

"That man is guilty as hell. He wouldn't leave my brother alone. Called him day and night, demanding Ainsley come over or do his wants at the drop of a hat. He was obsessed with Ainsley."

Thinking of the random phone call from the previous day, Blaine was intrigued and encouraged Monica to tell them more.

"He tried to have poor Ainsley killed at least once before," the man sitting next to Monica reported.

That again, Blaine noted.

"For clarification, you are?" Blaine asked the male speaker.

"Gene Bradley. I work with Monica."

"Okay," Blaine replied as he searched the list of

names and biographical information the desk clerk had ascertained upon the group's arrival. He had expected to find one male-sounding name on the list but noticed two possibilities: Gene Bradley and Steven Oliver. Blaine was curious, given that he only saw one definitive male among the visitors.

"How did you know Ainsley?" Blaine inquired, noticing that Phillips was being uncharacteristically brooding and tight-lipped.

"I met him and Conrad at a party Monica threw when they first arrived. Ainsley and I were both into record collecting and fantasy novels, so we hung out a lot. We hit the record stores every Wednesday evening after I got off work. Sometimes, when I went to get him, Rodney would be there, or I'd have to pick him up at Rodney's. Every time I saw that man, he gave me the creeps. He was always telling Ainsley when to be home and warning him about some serial killer murdering gay men in L.A. I don't think Ainsley believed there was a killer out there stalking gays, but he was always back when he told Rodney he would be. I asked him a hundred times why he cared so much what Rodney wanted, and he would just say it was easier that way."

"If he was scared of Williams, why did Ainsley not

stay with you, Miss Brown, instead of letting Rodney pay the rent on a place for him?"

"He hated that I live in the valley. His school was in Westlake, and he liked to go out dancing in Silverlake. He didn't want to commute from Reseda every day. Rodney has brainwashed our mom. She encouraged Ainsley to take Rodney's offer to get him a place."

"You didn't swallow the Kool-Aid?"

"Hell no," she responded angrily. "Rodney Williams is a con man and a snitch. He'd sell out his own mother if he thought it'd give him a leg up in the world."

"Why do you think he latched on to Ainsley, given Ainsley's lack of wealth or status?"

"Please, Detective," The redheaded woman to his left scoffed. "You're a man, and every man likes a piece of ass. Ainsley Brown was a fine piece of ass."

"What is your name?" Blaine asked, looking back at his bio sheet.

"Ask your partner. He knows," she saucily replied.

Blaine raised his eyebrows in interest as he stole a quick glance at the other end of the table. Phillips seemed to be abashedly seething. Blaine opted to follow that up later. "Sure, but for the sake of the record, could you tell me?"

The redhead took a deep sigh. "Stephen Oliver. Professionally, I'm known as Miss Leevah Lighton."

Blaine found the stage name amusing. It fit the woman. She was tall and thin with long, spider-like fingers and black-tipped nails. She was impeccably dressed in a rhinestone gown. It clicked for Blaine. She had probably gotten off work not long before coming to the police station. The other woman rounding out the group was a stout brunette, also adorned in evening wear and immaculately applied makeup. Blaine presumed from his list she was Billy Flynn, aka Candy Appel.

"So," he continued, addressing the room, "Rodney and Ainsley were?"

"Lovers," Leevah answered.

"Are you sure about that? My partner was told Rodney denied a romantic involvement with Ainsley."

"He always denies his relationships with his young men," Monica replied. "And he gets really angry if you even hint that he's gay. He had a year-long thing with Ainsley's friend, Carl. My brother said it was the worst kept secret in Westlake. I was on the phone with Ainsley when he had people over one night. I heard someone mention the name Carl, and then there was a lot of shouting. Ainsley said he'd call me back. Later, he told me Rodney had flown out of his seat, lunging at Ainsley's landlord. He tried to choke the guy until everyone else in the room pulled him off."

"Do you know who else was there that night?"

She replied in the negative.

"Miss Brown, was your mother aware of Rodney's relationship with your brother?"

"She would never have believed it, Detective. My mother refused to believe Ainsley was gay. Did not matter what she saw or heard, Ainsley was a saint to our mama, and saints aren't gay. Besides, I think she's at least half in love with Rodney herself. Every time he turns up in Chicago, she cooks for him, wears her best dress, and makes him the king of the castle. It's part of why I moved to L.A. in the first place. I wanted to go to nursing school as far from that b.s. as possible."

"Okay, but obsession doesn't always lead to murder," Phillips countered cautiously. "Did you say that Rodney tried to kill Ainsley before?"

Blaine was glad to see Phillips speaking up.

"He wouldn't admit it was Rodney," Monica replied. "Last year, he told us that someone, some stranger, attacked him on the street and stabbed him. But he told our sister Berenice back in Chicago that it was Rodney. And he lied about it to the police, He was terrified of Rodney."

"Did he tell any of you what happened that night?" Blaine asked.

"Only that he was walking home, and some stranger attacked him, stabbing him right there on the sidewalk while cars passed by," Monica answered. "But Berenice told me what Ainsley told her. It was not long after Ainsley arrived here to look at beauty schools. Rodney told him to stop by after he finished at the last school he was checking out. When Ainsley got to Rodney's apartment, there were three guys there. One of them went into Rodney's bedroom with him, and they closed the door. Ainsley wasn't sure how long they were gone, but when they came out, they were laughing, and the guy seemed to be counting what looked like five one-hundred-dollar bills. Ainsley said this made him uneasy, but he knew Alonzo Garcia, one of the other guys. He owns a limo and does a lot of favors for Rodney by driving people around.

"Rodney asked Ainsley to go with Alonzo to drop off the other two guys at the airport. He said it was late and didn't want Alonzo to go alone. So, Ainsley said okay. He was cool with Alonzo. The four of them then went to the underground garage beneath the apartment building. Alonzo got in the driver seat, and one of the strange men sat up front in the passenger seat. The other guy was getting in the back seat with

Ainsley, but he stopped and went to the trunk. Ainsley said he hadn't been paying attention, so he was surprised when that guy got in the car and started stabbing him with a small dagger. The other guys didn't move. They didn't even look back to see what was going on. Ainsley said he screamed out for help, but they just sat there. After the third or fourth jab, Ainsley was able to grab the knife and broke off the blade with his hand before he started having an asthma attack. It was then all three guys got out of the car and ran. They must have thought he was dying.

'Ainsley was able to drag himself out of the car and back to the elevator, but the asthma made it too difficult for him to call out for help. When the doors for the elevator opened, Rodney was standing there. Ainsley asked him to take him to the hospital, but Rodney took him up to his apartment and sat him in a chair while Rodney fixed himself a drink. Ainsley said he kept begging to go to the ER. He couldn't breathe. Rodney told him he would be all right. Ainsley finally faked the severity of the attack, which must have panicked Rodney into taking him to the hospital. Rodney drove him to the ER, took him inside, put him in a chair near the door, and drove off. It was a nurse who called the police after Ainsley's stab wounds had been treated. When he was released, Ainsley came straight home to Chicago."

"Did Ainsley ever explain why he would return here after that?" Detective Phillips asked.

"No, except Ainsley had made a lot of friends in California. He was very popular at a few of the gay bars, and I think he liked the scene in L.A. better than Chicago. He hoped to open a salon. He was really talented, but he didn't have any money. Rodney said he would pay for Ainsley's schooling, so maybe that's why he came back. I don't know."

"Did he make a police report?" Blaine inquired.

"He did," Gene remarked. "I was visiting him at the hospital when a couple of detectives came in to talk to him. He told them the story he told us about being stabbed by a stranger while walking home. At the time, I hadn't heard about what he told Bereniece, so I couldn't argue with him about it."

"Did any of you actually see or hear Rodney Williams threaten Ainsley, or did Ainsley tell any of you Rodney had hurt or threatened him?"

Dejected, the group acknowledged that none of them had, but each continued to insist that Rodney Williams was Ainsley's killer.

Blaine wished that obtaining justice was as easy as believing that someone was a killer, proof be damned.

The group stayed a short time longer answering questions. As they got up to leave, Blaine rose to show them out while Phillips stayed behind in the conference room to finish his notes. He nodded to each member of the group as they filed out.

"John," Miss Leeva said to him as she was going out the door, "When you talk to them, let Mom and Dad know I'm still alive. You know, in case they bothered wondering."

6

When Special Agents Bedding and Defonso entered the bullpen, they stood out among the city police officers plugging away at work. It may have been the matching dark suits the agents wore or their serious demeanor. It could have been the congenial-appearing man who stood between them. He was a tall, intelligent-looking man with a deep smile and tightly ringed curls of black hair.

"Detective Sergeant Blaine?" Agent Bedding asked before introducing himself and Defonso to the Sergeant and Detective Phillips. They were cordial and pleasant, as was the cleft-chinned man with them.

"Sergeant, Detective, this is Rodney Williams." The man with the agents moved forward and presented himself to the police officers, shaking their hands. A pencil-thin black mustache partially hid his wide grin, and large framed glasses obscured his eyes. Blaine immediately kind of liked Rodney Williams but was also acutely aware of the rumors that the man was a killer.

Agent Bedding asked if there was somewhere they could talk in private, and they were ushered into a conference room while Williams was temporarily left outside the door.

"We heard about the murder of Rodney's godson, Ainsley Brown," Defonso explained as the men took a seat around the table. "We also heard there might be allegations Rodney had something to do with it."

"His name has come up," Blaine shared cautiously.

Agent Bedding took a breath before saying, "Rodney has been an informant for us for a while now. It started when he contacted the agency about a potential robbery at LAX. Rodney had information on two men, Liam Edwards and Leroy Smith, a couple of guys he knows from various, um, enterprises."

"Rodney knows a lot of people," Defonso stepped in. "He will get you anything you need in the Rampart district or Koreatown. He's well connected and doesn't mind snitching."

"Right," Bedding continued. "So, he comes to us

and tells us that he's been asked to drive the getaway car in a heist at the airport. Most people aren't aware of how much money LAX makes in parking alone. They take in at least a hundred thousand a week just from the parking structures."

Phillips blew an impressed whistle while Blaine sat up and leaned forward in rapt interest as the agent continued.

"After it's collected, the money is taken by armed guard from LAX to be deposited. Rodney was friends with a guard, Liam Edwards. The plan was for Leroy Smith to "hold up" Edwards at gunpoint. He would then take the money and Rodney would be waiting nearby with the car."

"Yeah," agreed Bedding, "His info was good too. He gave us the time and date, and we forwarded the information to LAPD. Unfortunately for Smith, he tried to shoot it out with SWAT and wound up with a bullet in his spine. I think he's in prison now."

"Rodney let Smith get shot?" Blaine asked.

"Yeah," Bedding responded.

"Did Rodney plan the robbery?" Blaine countered.

"Probably," Bedding answered. "If you met Smith or Edwards, it's pretty clear they'd drown if they looked skyward during a rainstorm. No way either of them could set up a robbery."

"Initially," Defonso said, "Rodney went to the DEA with a case. He knew some guy that was a small-time drug dealer whose name he gave up. DEA picked up the guy but didn't take Rodney on as a paid informant. So, he contacted the FBI next."

"Rodney has been a good informant, and the FBI takes care of him," Defonso stated. "The FBI pays his rent and gives him some spending money. In return, he gives us info and perps. He's helped us put away some serious criminals."

"He's got eyes everywhere," Bedding chimed in.

"Well," Blaine said, "Let's meet this super spy."

Phillips showed Rodney into the room and sat him next to Blaine at the table.

"Detective Blaine." Rodney shook the cop's hand as he took his seat. He had a presence that filled the room. "Let me just start by saying that I am torn up by the death of young Ainsley. I want to help you find whoever it was did this to my boy."

"Oh, I'm sorry," Blaine baited, "I didn't realize Ainsley was your son."

"Not by blood, Detective, but he might as well have been. I've been helping to raise him since he was a teenager back in Chicago."

"Oh, are you from Chicago?" Blaine inquired.

"No, I'm from Louisiana," Rodney responded,

allowing his old Southern drawl to briefly creep out. "I used to travel a lot for work and spent time in Chicago. I met Ainsley's mama there forever ago and we became friends. Then, I met Ainsley and his sisters and felt the boy could use some masculine guidance in his life. Coretta Brown hasn't always had the best luck with men and Ainsley was growing up without a male role model."

Blaine briefly considered asking Rodney if he had been teaching the kid to write bad checks and possess illegal firearms, charges of which littered Rodney William's arrest record. "How long had Ainsley been in L.A.?"

"He's been out here a few months this time. This isn't the first time I've paid for him to come here. I've brought him, his mama and sisters out before and Ainsley was here earlier this year for a long visit."

"What did you guys do when Ainsley came to California?" the sergeant asked.

"When he was here last time, he was looking at beauty schools. It was his dream to open his own hair place. His sisters said he was really good at fixing up their hair and always did them up before they went out. He was here to go to one of those schools this time."

"Did you help him pay for school?"

"I did. No way that kid could have afforded it without my help. Those schools ain't cheap, you know. I told him to do his schooling in Chicago. It was less expensive there, for one thing. But Ainsley insisted on coming to California. He said it was here in L.A. where all the newest styles were happening and if he was gonna be any good, he needed to be here."

"I understand he had just graduated on the day he was murdered."

"Yes," Rodney agreed, "A few of us, his sister, some friends, and me, went to the ceremony, and then I took him and his friend Conrad out for a nice dinner to celebrate."

"What happened next?" asked Blaine.

"We were going to go out, maybe to a movie, but I could tell those young guys didn't want to get stuck with an old fart like me all night, so I told them I wasn't feeling like a movie and asked them to take me home."

"What happened when you got to your house?"

"They dropped me off and went out clubbing," Rodney answered. "Oh, hold up, Ainsley gave me a picture of him with Coretta. She had just sent it to him and told him to give it to me, and she'd get him another one when he got back to Chicago."

Blaine wondered if Rodney had slipped that tidbit

in to cover his own involvement or if it was an innocent detail. Maybe Conrad was mistaken when he said Rodney asked for photographs of him and Ainsley. The detective had not anticipated that Rodney would bring up the photograph and had been hoping to bring it up himself so that he and Phillips could assess Rodney's reaction to such information.

"You didn't ask for a photograph of Ainsley and Conrad?" He tested a little to see where it would go.

"Ainsley, sure, I got all kind of pictures of him through the years. I wouldn't want a picture of that other kid though. I didn't really know him."

Slick, thought Blaine, real slick.

"Did you hear from Ainsley again that evening?"

"No," Rodney responded. "I wish I had just gone with them. Maybe Ainsley would still be alive if I had."

Phillips looked at Blaine skeptically before Blaine went on, "Do you know who might have killed Ainsley Brown, Mr. Williams?" Blaine leaned in as he spoke so as to get a proper look at Rodney's face as he asked the question.

"Well, it coulda been anybody. You must know by now what Ainsley was. That kind of lifestyle will get you killed, won't it?" Williams leaned back in his chair, somewhat smug with his revelation.

Blaine was irritated with the comment, but he still

purposefully took the bait, "Do you think Ainsley was murdered because of his sexual orientation Mr. Williams?"

I'm not saying that," Rodney interjected with a smirk, "I'm just saying, being gay can you killed, can't it?"

"Have people tried to hurt you for being gay Mr. Williams?" Blaine posited, knowing he would get a rise out of the man.

"Now you look here detective, I'm no queer." The smirk had vanished and Rodney was visibly angered at the inference. "I didn't hold it against Ainsley. That was his business. But I'm not into that sort of thing."

"My apologies, Mr. Williams," Blaine said feigning regret. "I didn't mean to imply..."

"Rodney," Agent Bedding stepped in, "Do you know of anyone, specifically, who would want to hurt Ainsley? I believe you told Defonso and me about some guy you thought could have done it?"

"Yeah, you might check with Ronnie Hall," Williams said directing his attention to Detective Phillips. "He was the guy Ainsley rented a room from while he went to school. I had paid the boy's rent up through the end of the month, but Ronnie told him and Conrad they needed to be out tomorrow. I think he was pissed at the kid. Something about Ainsley messing around with some guy that was ol' Ronnie's boyfriend or some sort of thing."

"Is there anything or anyone you can recall who might want to hurt Ainsley Brown?" Blaine quizzed.

"No, I don't think so. Come to the funeral, though, detectives. Maybe his killer will be there, and you can catch the bastard."

The agents thanked Blaine and Phillips for the hospitality before leaving with Rodney Williams. Blaine leaned over and looked out the large conference window at Williams as he walked by. Williams turned slowly before beaming at him with a wide, toothy grin and a slow, sly wink of the eye.

7

Ronnie Hall was a small man with reddish-white pock-marked skin and a swagger that was contradictory to his lack of style and personality. He sat on the stained sofa in his office at the apartment building on Normandie Avenue. Smoke trailed from his clove cigarette, but he did not seem to be smoking it as much as holding it in his fingers for appearance's sake.

"Ronnie, I think you weren't truthful with me the other day," Phillips remarked from what may have been the only semi-clean chair in the room.

"I didn't lie to you, Phillips."

"I think you did. You failed to mention a fight you had with Ainsley just days before his death."

"An omission isn't a lie, Detective. It was so trivial, I forgot about the fight."

"Tell us about it."

"It was nothing. We had a disagreement over something."

"C'mon Ronnie, why don't you try again, and this time tell us what really happened."

Ronnie took a long drag off the cigarette. Blaine hated the smell of cloves but resisted the temptation to cough.

Fine. He came in to pay the rent for two more weeks. I told him I'd give the two weeks free if he did me a favor, you know? He told me to piss off like I was some kind of trash he could blow off like that. I told him he could get his shit and get out. I didn't want his rent. I'd seen the types of men and women he had coming and going from his place all the time. There was no way some of them wouldn't be interesting to the police. He got mad and said that Rodney had paid his rent till the end of the month and he wasn't leaving before then. I told him he'd find his stuff on the lawn, and he dared me to do it."

"Did you?" Blaine asked.

"Hell no. I wasn't gonna do anything to get Rodney involved. I owe him the job here."

"Rodney got you the job as landlord here?" Phillips clarified.

"Yeah. He owns the building with some friends of his. Last time I got pinched he bailed me out. He asked me if I wanted to do him a favor and take over here as the landlord."

"What was in it for him?"

"He needed a pair of eyes and ears on Ainsley."

"He wanted to keep tabs on the kid?

"Wouldn't you? He was paying for everything. That boy belonged to him."

"So, you got in a fight with your boss' boy?" Blaine was starting to see a picture emerging.

"Yeah," Ronnie replied nervously. "You're not gonna tell him, are you?"

"One never knows what will come out in the course of an investigation, Ronnie," Blaine answered with a shrug. "Tell me about the parties Ainsley threw."

"They weren't really parties. Ainsley just liked to have people over, you know? It was mostly people he knew from the clubs, his sister and some of her friends, and some of the people from his school and other tenants. People would just come over and hang at his place."

"Why did people like going over there?"

"Yeah," Ronnie remarked looking at Blaine like the detective was dumb.

Blaine returned the look with one of his own that seemed to convey what he was thinking, "Spill it."

"Ainsley had the best stuff in the city. And he was willing to share."

"Drugs?" Phillips said to clarify.

"What else?"

"Where was he getting it?"

"Rodney, I would guess. If you wanted to buy some from Ainsley, he could get it pretty quick. I always assumed he was getting it from Rodney."

"Rodney never offered or asked you to sell his stuff?" Phillips inquired.

"Nah, I don't think he trusted me all that much since I've been pinched for dealing."

"Did you meet Conrad Knowles?" Blaine cut in, changing the subject.

"Sure. He was the big, quiet kid from back east, right?"

Blaine nodded.

"Yeah. He was kinda a lump. When people were over, he would sit in the corner by himself or with Ainsley's sister. Sometimes, he would just go to the bedroom and watch TV.

"He kept to himself mostly. I heard him and

Ainsley arguing once in the bedroom. I came over to see what Ainsley had... procured... that day and walked in, but the living room and kitchen were empty. Then I heard their voices in the back room."

"What were they saying?" Phillips asked.

"I'm not totally sure, but it sounded like the Conrad kid was angry at Ainsley for partying all the time. He wanted to go back to Chicago and wanted Ainsley to go, too. Ainsley kept saying that he was staying in Los Angeles and Conrad was yelling that wasn't the plan. Then Ainsley stormed out and saw me there. I could tell he was pissed, but he smiled and got down to business."

"Interesting," Blaine mumbled before turning back to the landlord. "Out of curiosity, Ronnie, where were you when the murder happened?"

"I was out all night with friends and then met up with my girlfriend for breakfast at her work."

"Who is this girlfriend, and where does she live?"

"She lives here. Her name is Melissa Endicott."

BLAINE AND PHILLIPS left Hall's place and knocked on doors around the apartment complex, speaking with those who answered but failing to turn up new information. Blaine left a card at Melissa Endicott's apartment before the detectives made their way to Jerry's Famous Deli for a quick bite.

Blaine had stumbled on the venerable eatery several years before and spent many Sundays there with his wife and daughter in what were happier times. That chapter of his life was so far gone now, it sometimes felt like a dream—real but out of reach. His mind couldn't always recall the memories, but his chest always seemed able to remember the pain.

In a corner booth not far from the case of delectables, Blaine and Phillips lunched on Reubens and iced tea. Starving, Phillips was shoving fries into his mouth six at a time, but Blaine was too distracted to notice his own fries, let alone Phillips' behavior.

"What do we have?" Blaine asked aloud.

Phillips took a deep swallow before replying. "Well, we have a dead kid who, for all intents and purposes, was going somewhere in life."

"Right, but he was also dealing for Rodney Williams."

"Maybe he owed Rodney, or is that how Rodney got the return on his investment in the kid." Phillips postulated.

"That's definitely possible. It's too bad Liu's forensic research didn't turn up anything interesting. Or the autopsy. What do we know? Rodney does Ainsley and his family all of these 'favors,' and when the kid gets here, he's told he's going to work it off by selling Rodney's dope. Not a bad business model if you're Rodney Williams."

"Sure, but a drug deal gone bad could be what got Ainsley killed. We would have to find all his buyers, and I doubt he kept a list."

"What about Hall and his girlfriend? She didn't tell you about being with him when you spoke with her, and he's lied at least twice, that we know about."

"True, I'll get a warrant for the footage from that camera of hers." Phillips offered between bites of sandwich.

"You know," said Blaine as he absentmindedly twirled a fry in ketchup, "I'm curious about Conrad Knowles. He left out his own fight with Ainsley when I saw him in the hospital. Could be something there."

"True—or maybe Conrad wasn't a fan of Ainsley's new lifestyle as a drug dealer."

"He's definitely afraid of Rodney Williams. Maybe the drugs have something to do with it. I think I'm going to have to make a trip to Chicago to chat with him again and maybe drop in on Ainsley's mother."

"That will take a couple of days to get cleared. What do you want to do in the meantime?" Phillips asked.

"I think we need to go to a funeral."

8

As Blaine and Phillips approached the small church where Ainsley's funeral was being held, they were inundated with perfume from the scores of blossoms adorning the building's interior.

"I'm guessing all weddings in greater L.A. were canceled this week," Phillips whispered back.

"Seriously," Blaine concurred. "There's going to be a lot of angry bees."

The pair scanned the crowded pews before taking seats they believed would provide a modicum of invisibility from which to observe the mourners without the inconvenience of being inspected in return.

As he took his seat, Blaine continued to be perplexed

by the flower-to-mourner ratio. He counted less than thirty people in attendance, yet as he was counting the bouquets he was up to twenty before locking eyes with Rodney Williams. "Our cover's been blown," Blaine murmured as he nudged Phillips softly in the ribs.

Deliberately, Rodney sidled up the aisle. "Hello, detectives," he said through his wide, toothy grin. "Didn't expect to see anyone from the L... A... P... D... here. This is a nice surprise."

Blaine wasn't sure why the man had stressed each letter of the department's acronym as strongly as he did and found it off-putting and peculiar.

"Hello, Mr. Williams," Blaine greeted as they shook hands. "We wanted to pay our respects to the young man's family."

"Oh, I'm afraid I'm the only family the boy has here today."

"What about his sister?" Phillips inquired.

"Oh, she'll be along shortly, I'm sure. I just meant the only family that he could rely on to really look out for him, if you know what I mean."

"Enlighten us," Blaine replied.

"Well, a boy needs someone to take care of him, doesn't he? Like I said before, he didn't have a daddy, so someone had to help him along."

"And is that what you did, Mr. Williams? Helped him along, as you say?"

"I sure did. That boy was like a son to me. He was just a godson, but I loved him like he was my own child."

"You say, just a godson, how many godsons do you have?"

"Oh, a few here and there. There are a lot of young men out there that need guidance, and that's what I do, I guide them."

"Well, we're very sorry for your loss," Phillips mentioned.

"Say, Rodney, who sent all the flowers?" Blaine remarked as he motioned to the bouquets filling the room.

"I did," Rodney replied. "I wanted to make sure Ainsley had a proper send off and what better way than with a room filled with beauty."

"Rodney," a voice said quietly from behind Blaine.

"Oh, hello, Monica," Rodney said by way of acknowledgment. "People are starting to file in, if you'll excuse me." As he sauntered away, Monica Brown gestured for Blaine to follow her outside.

The day was crisp, and Monica shivered a little as she lit a cigarette and sat down near the church's small courtyard fountain. She offered one to Blaine, which he declined.

"This whole service is a farce, Detective," she murmured as she took a long, hard drag off the cigarette. "My mom will have a proper funeral for Ainsley in Chicago if his body ever gets there."

"Did she tell Rodney it was okay to have a funeral out here or did he do that himself?"

"She told him it was okay. She was never gonna argue with the *great* Rodney Williams. And, she needed some extra time to receive the insurance money so she could afford a funeral in the first place."

"Insurance money?"

"Yeah, I guess Rodney was up on Ainsley all the time about getting life insurance. He would tell my brother over and over that gays were getting killed left and right out here in California, and Ainsley needed to make sure our mom had the money to bury him when he got himself killed."

"That was thoughtful of Rodney."

"Wasn't it though?" She replied sarcastically.

"So, Ainsley took Rodney's advice and got a policy."

"Yeah. He told me he named our mom and grandma as joint beneficiaries so if anything did happen to him, she could use the money to help raise our younger brother, James. He's only ten and Ainsley was always worried that mom wouldn't have the means of providing James with better things than what we had growing up. He was a little obsessive about making sure James would have a good life."

"I see. Not to change the subject, but do you know who bought all of those bouquets in there?" Blaine asked. "Was it you?"

Monica coughed on the smoke she was inhaling and laughed.

"No sir, I don't have that kind of money. How much do you think a charge nurse makes?"

"Oh, you're a nurse?"

"Yep. Have been for about five years now at Cedars Sinai downtown. It's a fun job, you meet a lot of people that way."

"Speaking of meeting people, did you know a lot of the folks who hung out at Ainsley's place?"

"Those fools? No, not really. Ainsley would invite me over all the time so he could practice on wigs he put on me for his classes, but I didn't really know the other people that were hanging around. Most of them seemed to be Rodney's people."

"What do you mean, Rodney's people?"

"Well, he has a lot of people he claims to take care of. Most of them are young men with poor families. He swoops in and buys their affection. He's really just collecting people to do his dirty work. He calls them all his eyes and ears on the streets. Most, if not all, of the tenants on Normandie Avenue owe Rodney for something. So, he puts them in his building and uses them for info."

"Did he want eyes and ears on Ainsley?"

"I think a little, yeah. But he mostly wanted them on Ronnie Hall. Conrad was telling me that Rodney thinks Ronnie is up-charging on rent and pocketing the difference for himself. Rodney wanted Ainsley to find out what he could. So, knowing Ronnie liked to party, Rodney would give Ainsley drugs to loosen Ronnie up and get him talking. It didn't hurt that he was turning a tidy profit on all the others showing up at Ainsley's and buying that shit."

"So, the idea was that Ronnie would start coming to Ainsley for his fix and then start blabbing to him like they were buddies?"

"Exactly. Only problem was that Ainsley got along with everyone and didn't like being Rodney's messenger boy. So, if Ronnie was skimming, the chances of Ainsley telling Rodney were slim. He hated to grass someone up, and he seemed more loyal to his friendship with Ronnie than he did to Rodney."

"Conrad mentioned that he and Ainsley were

going to leave for Chicago the day after the graduation."

"That's news. My mom and James were coming out here in two weeks to celebrate Ainsley's graduation, so why would he go home?"

"Dunno, Conrad thought it was because Ainsley was afraid of Rodney and wanted some distance between them."

"Maybe. Ainsley didn't like Rodney like Rodney probably wanted him too, but Ainsley also wasn't gonna kill his golden goose, he wasn't dumb. No way he was going home without Rodney knowing about it, even if that's what he told Conrad."

"So, you think maybe Conrad had it wrong?"

"Not sure. Ainsley could be impulsive, so it's possible that he and Conrad decided on a whim to go back east. Then again, Conrad is a chicken. He was always afraid of something, so who knows if it was just his wishful thinking. He's only ever been comfortable at home with his mama, and he hated coming to California."

"I hear the organ playing," Blaine said with a strain of his ear toward the door.

Monica snuffed her cigarette with the toe of her pump, and they rushed back into the building hoping to sneak into their seats before the preacher began speaking.

"Anything good?" Phillips asked.

"Yeah, I'll tell you later."

"As long as you were gone, I assumed you had eloped to Vegas."

"Vegas is too crowded. We discussed Reno though."

"You don't like the mountains, all those critters, remember?"

Blaine's chuckling disturbed the people sitting around them and Phillips made apologies for their behavior.

The pastor took his place at the pulpit and was asking the small gathering to come together in prayer when the door opened again, and Steven Oliver stepped in.

He was tall and, like John, strikingly handsome. His bespoke suit let others know that he had taste. Money and arrogance all but dripped from him as he sauntered down the aisle. He seemed to be soaking in the attention provided by his late entrance until he came across his brother and Blaine. He opened his mouth as if to speak, then continued down the aisle with a low growl.

Phillips growled in return and turned away in annoyance.

"He looks good in a suit," Blaine whispered.

9

Phillips swallowed the whiskey remnants in his glass and walked over to the vending machine, where he bought a pack of Marlboros. Sitting back down he grabbed some matches from the bar top and lit a cigarette. For what felt like an eternity, the two cops sat silently staring at the bottles of booze lining the wall behind the bar.

Finally, Phillips looked over at Blaine as the latter sipped a Coca Cola and chuckling said, "It's a little sad that you've been reduced to tea-totaling."

"Someone has to drive your sorry ass home."

"Pfft. I could get someone in here to give me a lift."

"Want me to call your brother?"

Phillips glared at Blaine who smiled, amused with his own cheekiness.

Blaine knew he was poking the bear, but he was ready for his partner to get it out and get on with it. They had a murder to solve.

"So," Blaine prodded, "What happened?"

"Oh, you know, same old story. Parents raise three sons. Two become cops, the other comes out as gay and, on top of that, makes his living by performing in drag shows.

"He seems to be doing really well. The suit he wore to the funeral was impeccable."

Phillips released a deep sigh, clearly frustrated with Blaine's nonchalance.

"I guess he's doing all right. I haven't really spoken to him in the last twenty years. After he decided one Christmas to tell everyone he was gay, my father threw him out and disowned him. Told my younger brother Charlie and me that if he caught us speaking to Steven, we would be disowned too."

"So, you've steered clear of Steven to avoid ticking off the old man."

"Yeah, I guess. I also don't want any of Steven's fairy shit rubbing off on me."

"You know that's ridiculous, right?"

"I do. I just can't figure out what went wrong. We grew up in the same house. We had the same parents. We both played football and did Little League. We roughhoused and wrestled and were both altar boys. How did this happen to him?"

"I don't think being gay 'happens' to someone, John. I think it is just part of who they are. I have several cousins who are gay. I don't suppose they were struck with a radar gun that magically made them homosexual. That's just their wiring. Besides, what does it matter to me if my cousin Lydia prefers to date women? I'm not in the bedroom with them watching. Lydia hasn't called me up and said, 'Nick, critique my sex life and let me know what you think.' Even if she did, I would tell her it's none of my business. I have more important things to do than worry about whoever it is in her bed.

"Let me ask you, how does Steven's sexual preference really affect you?"

"I don't know," John replied, indicating to the bartender to bring him another whiskey. "It goes against the church, I know that."

Blaine laughed. "I haven't seen you go to mass in the twelve years I've known you."

Phillips quietly laughed as well before replying, "I never said I was a good Catholic."

"Given the number of women you've slept with, I think the church would spontaneously combust if you did attend."

Phillips lit another smoke as he continued to howl with laughter. "You know, Nick," he said after regaining his composure, "I think one of the biggest problems is that he never told me. We shared a bedroom growing up, and I had no idea. We double-dated to prom when he was a senior and I was a junior. He took the head cheerleader and everyone thought he was so cool. I thought he was so cool. I feel like he lied to me all those years."

"Maybe this is something you need to talk about with him?"

"Yeah, maybe. I'm not sure he would want to talk to me. Hell, I'm not sure we can talk without fighting."

"Maybe you can't. Who knows? Who knows anything? I thought I'd be traveling Europe with my wife or watching my daughter prosecute perps in court. Never thought in a million years I'd have to bury them both, thanks to Helen hitting the brakes on the 405 to avoid a freaking stray dog. I can't even blame the semi who plowed into them. How could I have seen that coming?

"I'd sure as hell love to talk to them again, and I would have liked to have seen my daughter raise her son instead of his father remarrying and raising the boy with his new wife. And believe me, I wouldn't care if Lynn wanted to marry a goat if I could have her and Helen back and get more time with my grandson."

Phillips ordered a whiskey for Blaine and the partners returned to silence as they ruminated on the casualty of chance and the happenstance of luck.

10

"Thanks for returning," Blaine said, shaking hands with Rodney Williams and his chaperones, Agents Bedding and Alfonso.

"When I got the call from your partner, Phillips here," Rodney said, nodding to John, "I wasn't going to say no to a request for my presence at the L... A... P... D."

Blaine inwardly cringed at the sound of Rodney saying LAPD in the staccato fashion he had used at the funeral.

"Detective Blaine," Rodney continued as they sat, "I'm afraid you think ill of me."

"It's awfully hard not to, Rodney," Blaine replied. "I've had half a dozen people tell me you murdered

Ainsley Brown, and you know, I'm inclined to believe them."

"Detective Blaine, do I look like a killer to you?"

There was a soft knock on the conference room door, and a secretary peeked her head in to beckon Blaine to come with her. Excusing himself the Sergeant left the room and took up the phone for the urgent call that had come in.

IN HIS ABSENCE, Phillips and the FBI agents bantered about the Dodgers and where the team would end up at the end of the season. Williams sat quietly listening without interjection until Agent Bedding asked him his thoughts on the team.

"Oh, if I were a betting man," he answered with a wink, "I probably wouldn't put my money on them. They have the pitching, but they're lacking hitters."

Defonso guffawed and defended the team. His temper flared a little at the mention of other teams who were better and he had started to raise his voice when Blaine returned to the room.

"My apologies, gentleman," Blaine said as he sat. "Where were we?"

"I had killed Ainsley," Rodney remarked.

"Are you confessing?"

"Not at all. You were accusing, remember? Detective Phillips, can you believe that your partner thinks I'm a cold-blooded killer?"

"Yeah, I really can." Phillips retorted. "Tell me again where you were when the murder occurred. You know, for curiosity's sake."

"I was at home, remember?"

"I can vouch for that," Agent Bedding cut in. "I called Rodney around 12:30 AM regarding a tip that he had called in. I wanted to let him know his information was good."

"Is that something you do often?" Blaine asked. "Call that late, I mean."

"If Rodney provided us with information that led to an arrest, we'll give him a call after and let him know he did good work," Defonso explained.

Blaine wondered if the agents were covering for Williams. So far, they had been amiable and forthcoming. But how far might they go to protect a valuable asset? The middle of the night seemed a weird time to pat an informant on the back.

"What did you do after the call?" Phillips inquired. "A 12:30 call would still have given you more than enough time to get to Normandie Avenue and shoot Ainsley Brown."

"It was the middle of the night, detective. I went to bed."

"Is there anyone who can place you at your house between, say, 1:00 AM. and 3:00 AM?"

"Yeah, a couple of my godsons have been staying with me. One of them just got out of jail, Alonzo Garcia. You know, maybe you should talk to him about Ainsley."

"Why is that?" Blaine responded.

"Alfonzo was pissed that Ainsley was living in what was his apartment. I hooked Ainsley up with it while Alonzo was locked up. When Alonzo got out, he wasn't too pleased that there was someone else in his space."

"You're saying your alibi could have been the killer because he didn't like the new tenant in his old apartment?" Blaine asked incredulously.

"Sure, why not? People have been killed for less."

Blaine had a feeling Rodney knew that last part all too well. Firsthand.

"If you don't believe me, you can always check the tape from the cameras on my house." Rodney offered. "I have them positioned on my front and back doors."

"We'll get that tape to you," Bedding cut in.

"No doubt after you've had a look to make sure your crow was in his nest," Blaine thought.

"Will that be all?" Rodney asked, starting to take his leave.

"Just one more question," Blaine advised. "How many life insurance policies did you have on Ainsley Brown altogether?"

For a brief moment, the oxygen left the room and none of the men around the table remembered how to speak.

Finally, Rodney answered. "Ainsley's mama was the benefactor on his life insurance. I think it was her and his gramma."

"But you had one too," Blaine replied as he slowly began to put the squeeze on the man.

"Well, now, of course, I had one to pay for the cost of the funeral," Williams replied. "I'd been telling that boy it was too dangerous here in L.A. for gays like him, someone was killing his kind. He must have thought he should do something in case I was right. Do you know the cost of burying someone, Detective? My uncle died a few years ago, and it cost over five thousand for his funeral. I told Ainsley that awhile back so I'm guessing he knew I couldn't afford that kind of money to bury him if he went and got himself killed."

"Rodney," Blaine said with deliberateness, "You and I both know there isn't anyone killing gay men out here."

"Isn't there?" Rodney asked coyly.

"So," Blaine continued, "I can understand a policy to pay for the funeral, but Ainsley is being buried in Chicago, and you have five insurance policies on Ainsley Brown. How many times were you planning on burying him?"

Blaine's eyes narrowed as he watched Williams respond to the revelation that Blaine knew about the multiple policies.

Phillips watched intently, knowing his partner would fill him in after the meeting.

"I don't know how you buried your loved ones, but I wanted to make sure mine got a proper send-off." Rodney stared at Blaine, daring him to go further. His burial remark wasn't lost on the Sergeant either. Rodney had done his homework.

Blaine wondered how much intel Rodney had gathered on him and Phillips over the course of the last couple of days.

"So, you needed five insurance policies to buy some flowers?" Blaine said with a turn of the screw.

"They were really nice flowers, Detective. Didn't you think?"

Blaine was amused. This guy was good.

"Who else do you have insurance policies on?" Blaine asked.

"I'm very popular, Sergeant Blaine. There are lots of people out there who would trust me to make sure they were properly buried."

"Or had really nice flowers."

"Flowers are important. Especially to gays like Ainsley. You know, that boy probably got himself killed for sniffing around the wrong man. Maybe he came across that serial killer I warned him about."

"We both know there isn't anyone out there right now pursuing young men and racking up the body count."

"Isn't there?" Rodney asked innocently. "I mean, Ainsley's dead. That's one."

"I imagine if such is the case, you should probably be careful." Blaine knew he was going to anger Rodney Williams. He did not expect the man to fly across the table at him.

Bedding and Defonso quickly grabbed Rodney and sat him back in his chair.

"That's the second time you've called me a faggot," Rodney spat at Blaine.

"First, Mr. Williams, I would never use that kind of language. Second, I didn't mean to imply something that you obviously find so... distasteful."

"I think we're probably done here." Bedding chimed in. He rose to leave. Defonso followed suit.

Gaining his composure, Rodney's smile returned. As he too stood, he said, "I'll give you another freebie, Detectives. You might consider looking at Randolph Barnes. He goes by "Duke." I've heard he's willing to do anything for enough money and he's in the area.

"Friend of yours?" Blaine questioned.

"We've met."

"Where do we find this Barnes?"

"Last I heard, he was in Long Beach. But I'd be quick if I were you. He doesn't stay in the same place for long."

"So," Phillips said as he and Blaine returned to their desks following the departure of Rodney and the agents. "Wanna fill me in?"

"I had an interesting phone call from one Irving Feffer at Equifax Insurance. He wanted to know if we had a suspect in Ainsley's case. Before I let him know what page we were on, I asked if he knew of any policies out there with Ainsley's name on them."

"And he came back with Rodney Williams as the beneficiary."

"Yep. On no less than five policies. There were six,

the last one was the one Monica knew about naming Coretta and Odette Brown.

"What is even more interesting," Blaine continued, "O'Connor told me he found nine more policies on individuals, including Rodney's brother and sister and several more 'godsons.' All of them with the same beneficiary in common—Rodney Williams."

"O'Connor was definitely interested when I told him that our suspect was none other than Rodney. He's going to freeze the payouts on the Ainsley policies, so it's going to be a long while before Rodney gets reimbursed for all of those flowers."

"In fairness," Phillips remarked, "He did want his family to have a beautiful service."

"I'm sure all the florists appreciated his generosity. I wonder how he paid for all of it."

"Drug money?"

"Maybe." Blaine agreed. "Or maybe drugs and insurance aren't his only rackets. The one thing that might work in our favor is I was able to get O'Connor to flag those policies."

11

After making the drive to Duke Barnes' last known address in Long Beach, Blaine and Phillips were feeling the heat of frustration.

"Alonzo Garcia next?" Phillips inquired as he sipped his coffee and stared at the Queen Mary in front of them.

Blaine liked to swing by the port and see the old ship whenever he was in the area. He didn't know why, but he felt a connection with the old girl, as though perhaps they were both relics of a bygone era. An easier era, maybe, when his life was polished and full of the promise of family and the means of being happy.

"Yeah," Blaine affirmed. "You know, there's an old

cargo ship over the way in San Pedro, I wouldn't mind being part of her volunteer crew one of these days if I ever retire."

"You want to be a deckhand on an old boat?"

"Look here, that old girl ain't no slouch. She served in three wars and took much-needed food and supplies to Europe and Guam during WWII."

"She really is an old girl in that case. Kinda reminds me of you, Blaine. She's been through the wars and still keeps on chugging along."

Blaine rolled his eyes and turned toward their car. "Hey, let's stop by Monica Brown's on the way to Garcia's work. I wanna see what she knows about Duke Barnes and his relationship with Rodney Williams."

"You have a soft spot for her."

"I do. I feel bad for the kid. You know her life in Chicago couldn't have been easy. Then she comes out here to make something of herself only to wind up with a dead brother and no answers."

Phillips nodded. He was feeling as anxious and frustrated as Blaine. They needed a big break in the case, and so far, they just kept hitting unraveled ends that went nowhere quickly.

~

WHEN THE DUO arrived at Monica Brown's apartment in Reseda, Blaine was not surprised to see a meticulously clean space. Given that Monica was a nurse he expected a certain fastidious nature to her home. However, there were knick-knacks, and the like that lent the little place a lived-in touch, and the smell of freshly brewed coffee was inviting.

"Officers," Monica greeted, "Have you come to tell me Rodney Williams is locked up?"

"No, we're still working on leads," Blaine replied as he and Phillips silently accepted her invitation to enter and sit. She brought in the fresh coffee and a few danish on a small plate adorned with yellow rose buds, which reminded Blaine of the dinnerware his daughter had received as a wedding gift from his brother. He stared at them a moment too long and was stirred from his memories by his hostess.

"Are you all right, Sergeant Blaine?"

"Yes, thank you. Monica, have you ever heard Rodney or Ainsley talk about a man named Duke Barnes?"

"Sure, he used to live on Normandie Avenue, next door to Ainsley. He was over at my brother's a lot when he first moved to L.A. Hang on, I think I have a picture of him."

Phillips and Blaine exchanged excited glances

while they waited for Monica to return from her bedroom with a photo album.

"Here," she said, pointing to a photo in the middle of the book. "That's Ainsley, Rodney, Conrad, and Duke Barnes."

"He's a handsome fellow," Phillips remarked, looking at the picture of a lithe, mustachioed Black man scrupulously dressed in the latest fashion.

"He is." Monica agreed. "Nice guy too."

"When was that photo taken?" Blaine asked as he peered at the eyes of Rodney Williams. Blaine could almost feel Rodney staring back at him and laughing.

"I dunno, maybe six months ago."

"Was this one of Ainsley's parties?"

"It wasn't one of those nights when people just showed up. It was Duke's birthday, and Rodney asked Ainsley to throw him a party. Duke and Rodney have been friends for a long time, I guess. Ainsley told me once that Rodney would tell him crazy stories about Duke making his money as a hitman, but I don't think anyone believed it."

"Why not?" Phillips asked, helping himself to a second danish.

"He is the nicest guy. Wouldn't hurt a fly. Like seriously, Ainsley found a spider in his place one day and yelled at Duke to kill it. Duke caught it up in a glass and released it outside. I think Rodney just liked to talk."

"Do you know what Duke does for a living?" Blaine inquired.

"Some kind of sales. He said his company sends him all over the U.S. He told me once they call him "The Closer" because he always gets the deal done," she said with a laugh.

"Monica," Blaine ventured, "Were you involved with Duke Barnes?"

The young woman blushed a little and peered into her coffee cup as she replied in the affirmative. "It was a short-term thing while he was here in L.A. He asked me out to dinner one night, and we had so much fun that when he was around, he'd take me out. He's very smart, Sergeant, and as Detective Phillips pointed out, not too hard to look at."

"What happened between you? Why did you stop seeing each other?" Phillips queried, still chewing some of his danish.

"He left Los Angeles. Actually, it was the day before Ainsley was shot. His job was relocating him to Florida for a spell. We parted ways on good terms. I told him if he came back to L.A. to look me up."

"What did Rodney think of your relationship with Barnes?" Blaine asked.

"I don't think he gave it a second thought if he ever registered it to begin with. If something didn't involve him or one of his 'boys,' he didn't much care, and given I'm a female, he really didn't care what I did."

"Not even to keep your mom up to date?"

Monica laughed heartily. "I doubt it has ever occurred to Rodney Williams that I exist, let alone that I'm Coretta Brown's daughter. That man doesn't give two damns about me. I'm not Ainsley, so I'm not shit to him."

"Do you, by chance, have any other photos of Barnes?"

"Sure."

Monica perused her photo album and plucked out several photos from its pages before setting them on the table in front of Blaine and Phillips.

"You can take those as long as I can have them back at some point," she offered.

"Thank you," Blaine replied, "I'll personally get them returned to you when we're done with them."

"He sure doesn't like to carry the same look twice, does he?" Phillips observed.

"Yeah, funny that," Monica remarked. "He was always mixing things up. I never knew who I was going out with until he knocked on my door. Sometimes there was a mustache, sometimes an earring.

One time he showed up here in a large afro wig and the sickest sunglasses. I thought he'd just walked off a Hollywood set."

"So, one might say he was a master of disguise," Blaine surmised.

"Absolutely," Monica agreed. "I used to jokingly ask him if he lived in a fashion museum or something. Honestly, at his place on Normandie Avenue, his entire spare room was full of clothes, wigs, shoes, and accessories. That man lives to look good."

"WHAT DO YOU THINK, NICK," Deputy Chief Chisolm questioned upon Blaine and Phillips' return from Monica's home to Rampart Division.

"I think Duke Barnes might well live up to his reputation as a contract killer. He sure does have a lot of costume changes and a long arrest record for someone who claims to be a salesman."

"If I were a hired gun, I'd probably have a number of get-ups," Phillips conceded.

"Yeah, I doubt a salesman needs false identities," Chisolm agreed. "When I was glancing at his file. I noticed that in each of his mugshots, he didn't have the same look twice. Taken out of context, you might not know those pictures were all the same guy."

"Not to mention he's been picked up and suspected of everything under the sun," Blaine added. "Robbery, discharging a firearm, unlawful possession of a firearm, attempted murder, assault with bodily injury, possession of an unregistered firearm, you know, the greatest hits."

"But never any time served?" Phillips asked.

"Nope, always seemed to get out of it."

"You know, Chief," Blaine said as he leaned back in his chair, "Both Duke Barnes and Rodney Williams are slippery suckers. They're clever enough not to get caught and not to leave anything behind. There are reasons they've been in operation so long."

"Yeah, I think you're right. Now that we know Barnes might be linked to this, let's get the paperwork filled out so you can go out to Chicago and run those mugshots by Conrad Knowles. Let's see what he has to say."

"Okay, Chief," Blaine replied.

"First though, go see Alonzo Garcia and see what he has to say for himself."

12

The air in the shabby tire shop where Alonzo Garcia was employed reeked of rubber and grease-stained cloth. Alonzo himself didn't seem to fare much better. He was a medium-sized man with cigarette-stained fingers, a catfish mustache, and eyes set too close together. He met with Blaine and Phillips at a small wooden picnic table that served as the employee lounge. The entire time he was with them, he stared at the ground as though his face had been drawn into that position and left that way.

Blaine wasn't sure if the guy was scared or just not very smart. Maybe both.

"Alonzo," Blaine started, "We're investigating the murder of Ainsley Brown. Did you know him?"

Alonzo shook his head, indicating that he was not familiar with the dead young man.

"What about Rodney Williams, do you know him?"

"Yeah, I know Rodney. I'm staying at his place right now."

"Why are you staying there?"

"I just got out of lock-up."

"What were you in for?"

"Drugs."

"Buying or selling?"

"Both, actually."

"But you're straight now and living with Rodney?"

"Yeah, he offered me a place to stay. He even picked me up from the joint when I got out."

"Are you and Rodney good friends?"

"I guess so. I mean, we weren't really before, but he's been cool since I got released. He told me to think of him as my godfather and that he takes care of his people."

"What was your relationship with him before like?" Phillips asked.

"I dunno. We know some of the same people, and sometimes I would buy drugs from him to sell."

"So, he was your dealer?"

"Kinda. It wasn't all the time though. Just when I couldn't get the stuff other places, you know?"

"We heard Rodney gets really good stuff." Blaine tossed out.

"Yeah, he does. That's why when I could, I would get it from him. It was worth way more money than the shit I could get from other places."

"What happened when you got picked up?" Blaine inquired innocently, aware of the answer from reading Alonzo's file and talking with Bedding and Defonso.

"You know," Garcia started, "I don't really know. This guy asked me if I could get him some smack. I said yeah, and after I got it, he turned out to be DEA. Next thing I know I'm pleading guilty and getting two years."

"DEA seems a bit extreme for a small fry like you. Why do you think they got involved?"

"Dunno. I think they thought I was in with some of the gangs and bigger dealers, but I was just getting it from whoever. I wasn't making a career out of selling dope. I just needed extra money here and there."

Blaine nodded in commiseration with Alonzo Garcia before asking him, "Do you, by chance, know Duke Barnes?"

Alonzo looked up for the first time. He clumsily

dropped the cigarette he had been holding and stared for a moment into Blaine's eyes.

"I don't mess with that guy," he responded.

"How so?" Blaine quizzed.

"Duke Barnes is serious shit. That man is the devil. Just saying his name makes me nervous."

"Why is that?"

"I've heard he's a hired gun. My friend, Woody, was almost killed by Duke."

"Woody?"

"Yeah, Woody Gilbert. He was married to Rodney Williams' niece, Ginny Williams. Yeah, Woody told me he was out one day mowing his yard, and this dude with big 'ol sunglasses and long hair walked up to him. As he was getting close to the sidewalk with his mower, the dude took out a gun and started firing. Got off three shots and then tore off in the opposite direction."

"How bad were his injuries?"

"One of the bullets missed him. One got him in the arm and the other in the hand."

"Were the police called?"

"Yeah, it was a big deal in the neighborhood. One of the guys who lived nearby, Willie, he saw Duke running up 104th Street. That's how we knew who it was that shot Woody up. Willie said that he probably wouldn't recognized Duke except that he seen him out drinking the night before with the same long hair wig and glasses on, and he even told Duke that he liked that look on him. Duke is well known around there. He likes one of the bars close to where Woody lives, and he's there all the time. Anyways, another guy, Allen something, he didn't see Duke, but that third bullet that missed Woody, it went through Allen's apartment window."

"Anyone know why someone would hire Duke Barnes to kill Woody Gilbert?" Blaine asked.

"Ginny Williams would want to hire someone. She hates Woody. After they got divorced, he quit his job so he didn't have to pay her any alimony or support his kids. He moved in with his mom and takes care of that yard all day. Ginny was pissed. Woody had a good job, and rumor was that when they got divorced, she was expecting a big payout from him. When she didn't get it, we all figured she was trying the next best thing, collecting on the life insurance that her Uncle Rodney insisted she get on Woody while they were married. Woody told the PD this when they were investigating, but he wouldn't admit that it was Duke trying to kill him. He was too afraid. Everyone around here knows Duke Barnes' reputation, and Woody knows that

Duke wouldn't have a problem taking another shot at him."

"Where is Ginny now?" Phillips wondered out loud.

"She moved to Louisiana, where her mom and Rodney are from. Monroe, Louisiana, I think."

"Did you tell all of this to the police?"

"Do you think I want Duke Barnes to kill me, Detective? I don't know nothing or nobody and that's my official story."

"And that includes Ainsley Brown."

"Yeah, I really don't know who that is. Should I?"

"I don't know. Rodney Williams thought you might know something about the kid's murder."

"Me? Like I said, I don't even know who that is. Why would I know something about his murder?"

"Beats me. Maybe Rodney just likes getting you pinched for things."

"He does? I'm not sure you can say that." Garcia said, lighting his third smoke.

"Alonzo, who do you think turned your name in to the DEA?"

Alonzo Garcia took a long drag off his cigarette as Blaine's words sank in and he realized what the cop was saying to him.

"Oh." Alonzo's eyes betrayed his growing fear.

"Indeed," Blaine remarked. He had a feeling Alonzo Garcia was telling the truth about not knowing Ainsley Brown. He also had a feeling that the kid had a reason to be scared. If Duke Barnes really was a killer, it was possible that Alonzo Garcia knew more than he should about Barnes' mercenary affairs.

"Just the same, where were you the night of July twenty-fourth?" Phillips interrogated.

"That was last Saturday? Let's see. I worked all day. Got off and went to Rodney's to shower and change. Nobody was there. I remember he left a note that he was at his godson's graduation. I went and grabbed a bite with my girlfriend and then we went to the movies and back to her place. I think I went home around midnight, maybe."

"Was Rodney there when you got home?"

"I guess so. His car was anyway. I must have assumed he was in bed. I didn't check to see or anything, though."

"You know, Alonzo," he said in a fatherly tone. "Maybe you should consider leaving town for a while. Until things in Ainsley's case are sorted out. Rodney fingered you for the killer and you're a little too close to Barnes' orbit. You got anywhere you can go, and quick?"

"I have a sister in Tulsa nobody knows about, and I get paid today."

"You got a car?"

"Yes, sir."

"Good. Get your check and go."

Garcia assured the detectives he would be in Tulsa within 24 hours.

Blaine hoped for Alonzo's sake that was enough time.

13

"Sergeant Blaine, I need your help." Rodney finished the last fry on his plate before moving on to his milkshake and sipping from it with relish.

Blaine had been suspicious when Rodney called him the day before asking for a meeting off police premises. Now, as he stared at his quarry from across the table, the detective searched to understand the mechanics behind Rodney's motive.

"Sergeant, if I'm a suspect in Ainsley's murder, so be it. In the end, you'll see you've got the wrong man. In the meantime, I believe I can be a valuable asset to you."

"You can? What can you do for me?"

"Thanks to your conversation with the insurance

people, they're refusing to cut me a check for the policies Ainsley had. I don't mind telling you that I need that money. I work hard for the FBI, but greasing the wheels of justice doesn't come cheap."

"So, you want us to get you the insurance money so you can share the love with your street informants."

"In a way. What I really want is a letter from the L... A... P... D... to the insurance company advising them that I'm not a suspect in the murder of Ainsley Brown."

"You want us to lie?" Blaine couldn't push down the involuntary chuckle.

"I don't want you to lie," Williams smiled surreptitiously. "I want you to tell the insurance investigator that I am not a suspect, and after the payout, you can investigate me all you want. In the meantime, I might know of a couple murders that would be very advantageous for you to solve. Could be very helpful to your careers."

"Mr. Williams, I can't issue such a letter. I believe you had Ainsley killed for that very money. Not only do we have five policies with you listed as the beneficiary, a witness puts you at the scene."

"I was at the scene. I got a call from a tenant in that apartment building telling me my beloved godson was dead. I hurried down there to see if it was true. When I arrived, you police were already there, so I stayed across the street out of your way. Is it illegal to stand on the street?"

"It is if you're there to make sure your hired gun got the job done this time."

"You have no idea the anguish Ainsley's murder has caused me. To see that poor boy shot up like that. It nearly killed me as much as it did to tell his dear mama what happened. He was like a son to me. Maybe you all need to get out there and look for witnesses more interested in helping you find the killer instead of grassing up an innocent man."

Blaine noted that Rodney ignored his remark alluding to the previous attempt on Ainsley's life.

"You know, Sergeant," Rodney continued, "How d'ya know that it wasn't those fags Ainsley ran around with that killed 'im? They all hung around him, trying to get to me and my money. Maybe they killed the boy as payback since I wouldn't let them in my house."

"Why wouldn't you let them in the house Rodney? All of the insurance policies you have out on various people tell me you like having a lot of people around. Maybe you liked having those friends of Ainsley's there too?"

Rodney's gaze changed for a split second, but as he was the consummate actor, he was able to quickly regain his composure. "You could write that information up for the insurance."

"Who did it, Rodney? Which of your criminal acquaintances killed that kid?"

"I would love to help you, *Sergeant* Blaine, but I don't see you sharing the favor and helping me out, and I don't do anything for free."

"You know Rodney, I imagine that's true," Blaine confirmed. "But you could give me that name and maybe cooperating with us could help you down the road."

"I already gave you a name," Rodney said as he sat back and took a drink of the coffee. He then looked Blaine up and down as though he were sizing the officer up to determine how much of a threat he might be.

"And where would we find this Barnes?" Phillips inquired.

"Detective, I've already said more than I should," Rodney replied, "Would you like me to solve your case for you too?" Rodney was amused with his own guile and couldn't help but giggle to himself. "Now," he continued, "how about that letter?"

"Mr. Williams, you will not be getting a letter from us unless it's to a judge asking him to disregard leniency when sentencing you for Ainsley's murder."

Rodney laughed at the Sergeant. It was a deep, guttural laugh that was somehow both genuine and forced. He then stood up and turned to the officer. "Thanks Blaine, I've enjoyed our time together. Good luck with your murder." With that, Rodney Williams strode out of the diner and out onto the street before disappearing into the pedestrians going by.

14

The flight to Chicago had been turbulent, but Blaine hardly noticed as he studied Ainsley's case notes. He hated to have any murder case dangling, unsolved, and waiting for justice. This case, in particular, bothered him. Rodney Williams had Ainsley Brown killed for those four life insurance policies, Blaine could feel it in his bones. He had been a cop long enough to know when his gut was right, and it was telling him Rodney was his guy. He was hoping that Conrad or Ainsley's mother, Coretta, might know something that could help, but he wasn't going to count on it.

The killer had been smart enough to wipe the scene of any clues. According to everyone who had known him, Ainsley Brown was a beloved member of the gay community in Los Angeles, a man without enemies. Thus far, all they had was four insurance policies, a previous attempt on Ainsley's life, an anonymous phone call, and a demoralizing lack of leads. Blaine hated the idea of anyone getting away with murder, especially since he felt Williams and Barnes had most likely done so before.

After his flight touched down, Blaine hailed a cab, but the snowdrifts that covered the city made navigation difficult for the driver, and he wound up dropping the sergeant off several blocks from his destination. Blaine fought against the biting wind as he trudged through the streets. The day was wet and desolate, bringing the city to a quiet hum rather than the normal noxious roar of people and traffic that often defined the local atmosphere. The entire Southwest area of Chicago appeared to be dodging the weather by wisely staying indoors. The whole city felt abandoned save for Blaine, who was seemingly the only person outdoors as he slogged his way toward the Auburn Gresham home of Conrad Knowles.

Blaine was aware of the reputation some of the neighborhoods in Chicago had for gang violence, so he proceeded with caution and purpose. Blaine rounded onto Aberdeen Street and found it to be a peaceful one, lined with pre-war bungalows and two-

and three-story apartment buildings. He had passed a quaint park on his way to Knowles' place and imagined that in better weather it would be a nice place to while away the day.

He thought about the phone call he made to Conrad advising of his trip to the Windy City and the apprehension Conrad had expressed at the idea of seeing him. Stammering and nervous, Conrad tried to persuade the detective to skip the trip altogether. When that failed, he made excuses as to why he wouldn't be home. Realizing that Blaine wasn't going to be moved, Knowles finally gave up and agreed to make himself available.

Upon his arrival at Conrad's house, Blaine rapped gently on the door. He didn't want to startle the jittery young man with any loud noises. A lovely woman near Blaine's age answered and identified herself as Conrad's mother, Beverly. Her hair was tied in a tight bun, and she wore a pair of gold-framed glasses. When she spoke, she was eloquent, and her voice was soft. "I'll let Conrad know you're here, Sergeant," she said, motioning for Blaine to take a seat. "He just got home from work and needed to freshen up."

Beverly Knowles disappeared around a corner and Blaine heard her tap on a door before telling Conrad his expected guest had arrived. She returned a moment later carrying a tray with a steaming kettle, cups, and cookies resting on it. She sat in a chair near the detective and inquired how he liked his tea. Quietly she brewed a cup and offered it to him before following it with the plate of cookies and a gesture for him to take some.

"How long have you lived here, Mrs. Knowles?" Blaine inquired in between bites of cookie.

"My husband, Bill, and I bought this house in 1973. Bill had just taken a job selling cars for Al Johnson and making enough money that we could finally afford a place of our own."

"I've actually heard of Al Johnson," Blaine remarked. "If I'm correct, he was the first Black man to own an auto dealership here."

"Yes, how does a middle-aged white cop from Los Angeles know that?"

Blaine laughed softly. "I'm a bit of a history buff, have been for years. I hope to open a museum about the LAPD someday."

"I wish you luck with that, Sergeant. It sounds like quite the endeavor."

"I imagine it will be. Tell me, does your husband still work for Mr. Johnson?"

Beverly shook her head, "No, Bill died last year of cancer." Her eyes saddened as she relayed the news and looked out the window next to her for several moments as she gathered herself.

Conrad entered the room and broke the silence. He smiled wanly as he shook Blaine's hand and sat down in a chair near his mother. As he did so, Mrs. Knowles excused herself, nodding to the detective, who told her he was happy to meet her before thanking her for letting him into her home. She smiled and returned the cordiality as she left the room and again went down the nearby hallway.

"How are you, Conrad?" Blaine asked as he set down his cup.

"Okay, I guess," he replied. His eyes were dark and sallow, and he looked as though he hadn't known sleep for years.

"Are you sure you're okay?" Blaine inquired.

"Yeah, I'm okay." The answer was quiet and uneasy as Conrad cast his eyes toward his wringing hands. "They're out there all the time, you know," he motioned his head toward the window. "They're not now, but they usually are."

"Who?" Blaine asked as he instinctively moved forward in his seat.

"I think they're Rodney Williams' people. I don't know for sure. Do you see that little wall across the way, in front of the house on the corner?" Blaine nodded that he did. "That is where they usually hang out. One of them lives in that house with his folks."

"How do you know they're interested in you?" Blaine asked.

"I don't for sure," Conrad admitted. "But they stare at me and yell things at me. They call me a fag and pull back their coats to show me they have guns. I try to avoid them. I sneak out around the back past the garage to get to my car out on the street. When I get home, I don't leave again until I have to be back at work. Do you know what kind of life that is, Sergeant?"

Blaine genuinely felt bad for the young man. Conrad was in his twenties. He should be out and enjoying his life, meeting people, and being carefree.

"Have you called the police?" Blaine inquired, knowing there would be little the cops could do. "About the firearms, I mean."

"My mom has. She doesn't like them out there, and my younger brother hollers back at them and causes trouble. He's not afraid, but he should be. My mom has called three or four times, but someone must be tipping them off 'cause each time they've been gone before the cops arrive."

"Well," Blaine replied, "One way we can stop them is by putting Ainsley's killers away."

Conrad stared down at the floor at the mention of his dead friend.

"You saw the shooter, Conrad. Do you think you can identify him?"

"I don't know," Conrad remarked cautiously, "It was dark out, I don't think I can really help."

"Let's give it a try," Blaine opened the bag he had brought with him and took out a photo album. It was a standard six pack photo lineup, filled with the mugshots of possible criminals readily available for identification.

"Have a look through these and tell me if you recognize anyone," Blaine said as he handed Conrad the small book.

"Okay," Conrad agreed, "But I doubt I'll know anyone." He took the book and began to flip it slowly. Blaine watched Conrad's face intently as the younger man slowly gazed at the pictures. When he flipped to the page containing the photograph of Randolph Barnes, Conrad Knowles began to visibly shake. He stared at the picture, his eyes large and scared.

"Do you recognize anyone?" Blaine questioned, his insides churning with nerves and hope.

Conrad's voice cracked as he responded, "I thought I did for a moment, but I do not."

Crestfallen, Blaine asked, "Are you sure?"

Conrad paused. His silence once again caused Blaine to wish the kid would point at the picture of Randolph Barnes. But Conrad shook his head and said again that he did not know anyone in the photographs. Somewhat briskly, he finished flipping through the other pictures, then handed the book back to Blaine and stood, indicating he was done talking.

"Thank you for coming, Sergeant. I'm sorry you came all this way for nothing."

Blaine held out his hand and shook Conrad's as he said, "It's okay Conrad. If you change your mind or think of anything, let me know right away. Here is my card. I've written my direct extension on it."

Conrad's hand trembled as he took the card and put it in his pocket. He then walked the Sergeant to the door and stood behind it as he let Blaine out of the house and back into the cold.

The detective looked about and saw there were now three tough looking men sitting on the wall as Conrad said they would be.

As for Conrad, he shut the door behind the detective without uttering another word.

Blaine noticed the lights in the front of the house were turned off as he made his way down the walk and toward the main road where he could get a cab to his

hotel. He made a surreptitious look at the men gathered on the corner, noting two appeared to be working
hard to look menacing. Blaine was somewhat
bemused by their behavior but kept to himself as he
walked toward the main road to find a cab.

15

Coretta Brown's eyes reflected her anguish. She stared ahead at the lake with Blaine sitting next to her. He, too, pondered the agony of loss. Time filled the expanse between them until Coretta began to speak.

"Detective Blaine, I will try to be as nice as I can, but I need you to get a few things straight. This hogwash about Rodney Williams being my boy's killer is something I cannot abide. Rodney loved my boy as though he was his son, and he has taken care of Ainsley and me for years."

"Mrs. Brown..." Blaine started.

"Detective, when Rodney called me to tell me about Ainsley, he was as brokenhearted as the rest of us. I'd just had surgery, so I could not travel and be there for my boy's funeral in California, but Rodney took care of everything. A few of Ainsley's friends called me and said the service was the most beautiful they had ever seen. People don't kill a boy and then lavish them with a beautiful service like that."

Knowing the opposite to be true, Detective Blaine bit his tongue and stared ahead at the boats on the water. He and Detective Phillips had spoken with Ainsley's sister. By her account, Coretta was not pleased that Rodney Williams was the main suspect. Now, he was sitting next to her on a cold bench, looking out on Lake Michigan.

She was a small woman, not quite five feet tall and very thin, but she had the presence of a lion. Blaine could tell she was formidable before she had uttered a word.

"My daughter told me she spoke to you and your partner, Detective."

"She has," Blaine replied.

"And I've heard that Mr. Williams is your main suspect."

"He is."

"Rodney Williams is a brother to me. He was a brother to my Ainsley. My son looked up to Mr. Williams, and for the last ten years, Mr. Williams has been a mentor and a guardian angel to Ainsley. The whole Williams family loved my boy. So much so Rodney's own sister, Eugenia offered to adopt him when he was younger. Obviously, that wasn't an option for her since he had a mother, but that's how much they loved Ainsley. They wanted to legally make him part of their family. Would a man kill someone he loved like his own?"

"He might."

"Mr. Williams is no dog. Whatever you say, that doesn't change my love for him."

Switching gears, Blaine cut in, "Where did your family meet Rodney?'

"At church," Coretta replied. "Rodney Williams was in Chicago for work and liked it so much he would come and stay for months at a time. He came into our church one Sunday. He said he had heard good things about our pastor, Brother Lewis. Rodney said the church reminded him of the one in Louisiana where he grew up. He stood up that first day and testified before the Lord and everyone else. After that, he became a regular in our congregation. He immediately took a liking to Ainsley, and they became fast friends."

Blaine thought a moment before gently asking, "If it was about ten years ago that you met Rodney, would that have made Ainsley about fifteen years old?"

Coretta instantly prickled. "Detective Blaine, do

not go getting any ideas in that head of yours about my boy and Mr. Williams. I know you are trying to match up my son with some kind of homosexual activities. If that isn't the first question you've been asking people, I'll be damned it's the second one you ask, and I am telling you, my son was not gay."

Blaine again bit his tongue.

"Now Rodney, he was very supportive of Ainsley in whatever he did," she continued. "You know, nearly ninety-eight percent of Ainsley's clothes were purchased by Mr. Williams. Ainsley was a very neat dresser and a lot of his friends hated that he had nice new things and they didn't. They would say things about him and tease him about it. Not Mr. Williams, he gave the boy money so he could look nice. He also paid for all of Ainsley's living expenses here and in Los Angeles, and he took care of Ainsley's beauty school payments. Even now, he helps me. If it wasn't for Rodney Williams, I don't know what I would do. Ainsley's dad left us when he was a baby, and my second husband hasn't been around in years.

"Perhaps you don't want to hear these things, Detective, because they are all good things about Rodney. I'm sorry, but I can't help you in the bad department about him. We don't have one of those departments in our hearts like you do."

"Mrs. Brown, I am not trying to make Rodney Williams look bad. I'm not trying to be villainous, and I'm not trying to go after Mr. Williams for no reason. On the night Ainsley and Conrad were shot, Mr. Williams was one of the first people on the scene. There were five insurance policies in your son's name, and all but one had Rodney Williams listed as the beneficiary. On one of them, the signature didn't quite match up to the others, as if it had been forged. He attempted to have Ainsley killed once before in the parking garage of his apartment building, and he knows people capable of murder. I am not totally committed to the fact that Mr. Williams is your son's killer, but I need to catch whoever the killer is. It is a fact that somebody killed your son by gunning him down in the middle of the night. He had his whole life in front of him. Unfortunately for Mr. Williams, he has the greatest motive, and his reputation in Los Angeles is not the same as the one he has with the Brown family."

Coretta Brown sat quietly for a moment. She believed that Detective Sergeant Nick Blaine wanted to find her son's killer. She could tell he was earnest and determined, qualities she liked about him. But she still could not endure him believing that Rodney

Williams was the scoundrel he was making him out to be.

"I don't know why Ainsley had multiple life insurance policies, but I do know that if he did, it must be what Ainsley wanted. I knew about the policy with his grandma and me listed on it, but other than that, do you think my son would discuss any of his business? Rodney told Ainsley he had a bright financial future. You act as if Blacks can't have good, sound financial futures and support each other."

Blaine started to speak, but Coretta held up her hand and continued, "I asked Rodney to let me pay for Ainsley's insurance policy, but he wouldn't hear of it. He said he was going to take it out of the allowance he gave Ainsley, and once Ainsley was done with school, he could pay all his own expenses. When Ainsley went out and got money orders to pay for that insurance, Rodney found out and told him to stop doing it and save his money."

"Do you know if Rodney paid for Ainsley to come to Los Angeles?" Blaine asked as he ignored the inference that he was racist.

"Rodney wanted Ainsley to stay here in Chicago and finish school," Coretta answered. "Rodney told my son he would pay for it, but Ainsley wanted to go back to Los Angeles and be around those two-faced people there."

"Do you know who the two-faced people were, Mrs. Brown?"

"All of those so-called friends who said behind his back that Ainsley was homosexual. They pretended to be his friends, and then they would tell anyone who would listen that my boy was gay."

Blaine quickly weighed the pros and cons of telling Coretta Brown that her son frequented gay bars, about Conrad, and about Ainsley's friends who had come to the station and talked about him, including that he was gay. He also wondered what she would say to him if she knew Rodney Williams had told Ainsley not to come to L.A. because someone was killing gay men. However, before he could say anything, Coretta spoke again.

"Rodney and Ainsley—they always went to church, and those so-called friends of Ainsley's were mad because Rodney was taking Ainsley away from them. You use your authority to gain information that isn't true, but you haven't been lucky, have you? Have you ever thought of looking at Ronnie Hall? He was not a friend of my son, not the way he did him in the last two weeks Ainsley was there."

"What happened between Ainsley and Ronnie

Hall?" Blaine wondered if she knew something he hadn't yet been told.

"During the week of Ainsley's commencement exercises, Ronnie Hall kicked my son out of his apartment, even though Mr. Williams had told me he paid the rent for the whole month. Ronnie Hall was angry with Ainsley. Do you call that the act of a friend?"

"Do you think Ronnie Hall could shoot Ainsley?" Blaine asked.

"I think people can do all manner of things," Coretta replied.

"We looked into Mr. Hall," Blaine told her. "He has an alibi for the time of Ainsley's death."

"Convenient for him," Coretta replied glibly. "I hope you find who murdered my son, Detective Blaine, and I hope you stop spinning your wheels on Rodney Williams and start looking for the real killer. I know you told the insurance not to pay Mr. Williams on my son's behalf. But the oppressed will win. Mr. Williams paid to have my son's body returned here to Chicago. He took care of most of the arrangements and paid for both funerals.

"I'm leaving for my daughter's home and to have another surgery in a few weeks. Please do not call me there and get me upset. I want my son to rest in peace, and I know that right now, he's not resting because of all this business with Rodney. God will take care of everything in the end, and you'll see that you were wrong about Mr. Williams."

Coretta stood up quickly and with purpose. She did not wait for Blaine to get on his feet. She skipped the usual niceties, choosing instead to walk away.

Blaine stayed awhile longer staring out at the boats on Lake Michigan.

THE FLIGHT back to Los Angeles was interminable for Blaine. The detective was disheartened following the encounter with Coretta Brown. Her contempt continued to sting, but not as much as her unwavering faith in Rodney Williams.

Williams was affable and manipulative, which was apparent from the outset. But his ability to thoroughly delude the Brown family was grating. Blaine felt sorry for Coretta. Not the Coretta he met a day ago, but the Coretta of the future, the one who would someday realize the many ways Rodney Williams had lied to her before and after he engineered the death of her elder son.

The hum of the plane lulled him toward sleep as his thoughts turned to Beverly Knowles. While

Coretta was determined to stand faithfully by her son's presumed killer, Mrs. Knowles lived each day with the fear that same killer would come for her son. Her stoicism was in stark contrast to Coretta's stubborn support of Rodney Williams. Blaine wondered if Coretta Brown would still be inclined to defend Rodney if she had seen the mugshot of Duke Barnes. He tried to show it to her when they met, but Coretta refused to look. She told Blaine she would "play no part in his effort to ruin Rodney's life."

HOURS AND MILES passed as he napped off the stress of the case. Upon landing, he was jarred awake and became acutely aware that he could use some coffee and a breath mint or two.

It was early afternoon when he finally walked out of LAX, happy to see Phillips languidly leaning on the side of the car.

"Did the villagers run you out of town with pitch-forks?" he asked through a Pink's hot dog while nodding to the cup of hot coffee and bag of food resting on the roof of the vehicle.

"Your waist called. It wants your old measurements back." Blaine retorted, thrilled that his partner knew exactly what he needed.

In the car, Blaine apprised Phillips of what had transpired in Chicago.

Phillips had heard it all during the phone call Blaine had made to him the night before but listened intently. The rehash of the trip's events caused the drive back to Rampart Division to pass quickly.

"Oh," Phillips said as he tossed a file onto Blaine's desk while sitting at his own. "We got the handwriting analysis on that fourth insurance policy. The expert is certain the signature matches the writing samples we gave him from Rodney's file. He is absolutely sure that the signature was not made by Ainsley."

"Williams probably had Ainsley sign the other three and then used those to forge the signature on the fourth."

"That would make sense, hard to prove though."

"Hey," Blaine exclaimed, sitting up in his chair. "Remember that story the Feds told us about Rodney and the LAX robbery?"

"Yeah."

"Wouldn't you think that at some point, the man Rodney framed would have asked himself how the LAPD was there that day?"

"I know I would have," Phillips concurred. "And, if

I were him, I would want to know where Rodney Williams was while I was being shot at by SWAT that day."

"Defonso said Smith asked Rodney to drive the getaway car. You've read Smith and Edward's files, anything about those two geniuses that would make you think they could plan something as complex as an armed robbery?"

"Not even a little. I'm not sure those guys would be smart enough not to drown if they looked up in a rainstorm."

"Right. I think I'm going to pay Mr. Smith a visit."

16

Los Angeles April 1977

Rodney had a reputation as a guy who could get things and knew people. Whatever you needed, Rodney could hook you up, and once he had, you owed him.

Liam had struggled for years to find employment gainful enough to support his girlfriend and three kids. He had spent a decade in low end jobs and working for Rodney Williams here and there for a pittance. It all amounted to little on the kitchen table and less by way of ego stroking. He felt that he had finally made it when he got a job working for an armored car company. When Liam told Rodney about the job he was also excited, especially when he heard that in a good week Liam could be handling up to $150,000.

Leroy Smith on the other hand wasn't having the same luck and 1977 had been a particularly difficult year for him. He was out of work, out of money, and out of prospects. He was nearing the end of his rope when he attended a party at his friend Ronnie Hall's.

The music was ear-splitting that night in Hall's apartment, but nobody but the neighbors cared. Infused with cocaine and rum sweat poured off of Leroy as he gyrated through the crowd of people stuffed into the tiny living room. He was determined to ignore his plight and spend the evening forgetting that he would be homeless in two weeks time. He had caught the eye of a cute girl who had been provocatively sidling toward him. If he didn't have a job or a home, at least he might get lucky. It was then that a tall man with a cheshire cat grin sidled up next to him and said, "I hear that you're in need of some work?"

"Oh, hey Rodney, it's been awhile."

"It has Leroy, but you are just the man I was hoping to run into night. Let's talk."

Leroy followed Rodney out of the apartment, down the stairs, and into the complex courtyard. They sat down on a bench when Rodney lit a cigarette that he then handed to Leroy before doing the same for himself.

"Where have you been man?" Rodney asked.

"I got a dime for robbery."

"Right, I thought I had heard something about that. What happened man?"

"A jewelry store. My girlfriend worked there and promised that it would be an easy score. She had the code to the safe where the owner stored everything and the code to the alarm. All I had to do was go in, turn off the alarm, and then empty the vault. At the time I knew a guy who could help me offload everything so I had it all worked out. I didn't count on her banging her boss though and he was stealing from himself. She set me up. I took the jewelry, he turned in the robbery for the insurance money, and then she phoned in a tip that told the LAPD exactly where to find me."

"Damn!" Rodney exclaimed. "That's a tough break. You been working since you got out?"

"I was for a bit at donut shop, but I got fired for showing up late and nobody wants to hiring an ex-con."

"Yeah, I know how that is. Lucky for you, I might know of some easy work you could do."

"Yeah?"

"I have it on good authority that the parking at LAX is lucrative."

"How?"

"Where do you think all that money from parking goes? Think about all the people coming and going and all the money they're ponying up."

"Sure, but what are we going to do about it?"

"So, I know the guy who in charge of collecting the money and taking it from the airport to the bank in an armored vehicle."

"There aren't two guys?"

"Sure, but we only need one. Every week attendants have collected the money from the booths throughout the airport. Each time they do they take it to the cashier's office where it is deposited into the safe for the Friday pick up, that's when my guy picks it up and takes it for deposit at the bank. Only, maybe he doesn't make it to the truck?"

"Right," Leroy said as the picture started to become clear for him. "So what do you have in mind for me to do?"

"You're the guy who intercepts it. Our guy is in on it, so you just have to pretend that you're holding him up. He gives you the money then you hightail it fifty yards to the car where I'm waiting. That's it."

"Why not just sub out the bags with similar ones so that a stick up isn't even needed?"

"It won't work, the bags are specially marked by the airport and no two bags are the same. C'mon, whatdaya think?"

"When do you want to do this?"

"One month from now. We'll spend the next few weeks laying out our plan and rehearsing to hash out any kinks."

"I'm in." Leroy didn't bother to ask any more questions. He probably should have. Rodney's heist was simple and guaranteed no jail time, as long as you weren't Leroy Smith or Liam Edwards.

Leroy returned to Ronnie's elated. He was going to make an easy score in a week's time he would be set with enough to put a deposit down on a nice place and even get a car. That night he danced until his legs hurt and then took the cute girl home for the best one-nighter of his life.

THE MORNING of their heist Liam was nervous. Rodney had promised him that he wouldn't be implicated and would be able to get cut in on their take and keep his job. His hands shook as he put on his uniform's tie and he felt like he had an avocado pit knotted in the bottom of his stomach. He had been sweating profusely for six days and as exciting as Rodney made it seem, Liam just wanted the day over.

Leroy on the other hand woke up singing and was an hour early to Rodney's place. He was excited for his new life. Rodney was also in a good mood. He met Leroy at the door with a hug and smile exclaiming, "In a few hours we're going to be set for a long to come my friend!"

Rodney handed Leroy a .38 revolver saying, "That's loaded, so be careful. Don't go shooting your dick off." Rodney laughed at his own joke.

"Does it really need to be loaded?" Leroy asked.

"Yeah, why not? We want to give our robbery a sense of authenticity, don't we?"

"I guess so." Leroy answered as he stuck the gun in the waistband of his pants. "Should we get going? It's getting near time."

"Sure." Rodney answered. "You go ahead and get in the car, I need to grab my wallet from the other room."

As he walked out, Leroy thought he heard Rodney speaking with someone else, but he was too nervous and too energized to care so he made his way to the parking structure and got comfortable in the passenger seat of Rodney's car. A few minutes later Rodney joined him and starting up the car he clapped his hands together and shouted, "Let's go!"

Both men were highly ebullient as they made their way out to the airport. By the time they arrived at the designated point, Leroy was practically bursting at the seams. The reality of their endeavor was beginning to sink in which was daunting to him considering the consequences should they be caught.

"Deep breaths," Rodney assured him. "Just take deep breaths, and keep your eye on the prize."

Leroy nodded as he got of the car and slowly made his way to the spot on Liam's route that they had deemed the best place for the confrontation. Having spent much of his youth pilfering from stores and casually selling drugs, Leroy wasn't new to criminal pursuits, but this, robbing LAX, this was a whole new realm of malfeasance. As he got into position the enormity of the task gave him shaky hands and wobbly knees. A moment later Leroy heard a long whistle, the indication from Liam that the plan was in motion.

Leroy counted to twenty as he had done when they rehearsed the robbery. He could feel the perspiration beading along the follicles of his hair and mustache. His thin and wiry frame felt smaller than usual and he was having a hard time taking air into his lungs. He peered around the corner and saw Liam coming toward him with the satchel in hand. He paused a few more seconds before sliding out from behind the wall that had hidden him and shouting, "Stop! This is a stick up!"

Leroy was disappointed with his choice of words. He had practiced what he would say at that moment, standing in the front of the mirror with his chest puffed up and his shoulders back. He had seen enough films to know the cliches he wanted to avoid when the time came , he had spent hours staring at himself, wildly rehearsing tough sounding phrases parsed with modern lingo. When he heard himself say, "This is a stick up!" he half hoped that his partner hadn't heard him, but, he had.

Liam dropped the satchel to the ground and raised his arms over his head just as he had done when they had prepared this moment. He earnestly stared at Leroy waiting for the next command to get on the ground. Yet, before the words could be uttered his dark eyes grew fearful and he quickly moved his tall, lanky body into a kneeling position on the ground, keeping hands behind his head. Leroy watched Liam's actions in confusion as he failed at first to register the shrieking and clamoring around him. It took several moments before he understood the words bellowing at him from all sides:

"LAPD! GET DOWN! GET DOWN ON YOUR KNEES AND PLACE YOUR HANDS ON YOUR HEAD!"

Leroy realized that they were encircled by a SWAT team and he could see the guns peering over official vehicles at him. In a flash, Leroy decided to ignore the shouts from the leading officer and rather than kowtowing to their demands he believed he could make a run for it. Pretending that he was going to lay down his weapon, Leroy began to lower his arms which he had raised out of instinct once his brain had discerned what his eyes were seeing. Yelling back assurance of compliance to the officers he appeared to be bending his body toward the ground before he instead fired his gun toward the officers before trying to run back toward his starting position and the safety of the cement wall he had previously used for hiding.

For a moment he had believed he was going to get away, but that feeling of freedom and exuberance dispelled as a stinging heat pierced his lower back and felt himself falling toward the pavement. Leroy could feel the hole in his back and the blood gushing forth, but the pain was so severe that in a few minutes he couldn't feel anything but a white heat.

Days later he gained consciousness, chained to a hospital bed.

At the end of the bed Leroy spied legs protruding from beneath a newspaper and in a small raspy voice he squeaked, "Where am I?"

The corner of the paper momentarily crumpled behind which Leroy could see a large, thick mustache and the outline of a badge. "You're at a pit stop on your way to prison."

17

Los Angeles July 1984

"Here is the report on Rodney Williams' finances," Phillips remarked as he flopped a file in front of his partner. "According to this, he needs money. He's in debt to multiple credit card companies and owes thousands to some suit maker in the Valley. The FBI is paying his rent, but with his spending habits, I can't imagine the extra money they're giving him is going very far."

"The money he could make on those life insurance policies would more than cover his debts with plenty left over," agreed Blaine.

"Some of these debts are in collections," Phillips noted. "I can see why he might have felt desperate enough to cash in those policies. Given his financial history, I wonder if this is the first time he's pulled such a scheme. If not, who were the other victims?"

"Well, we know that he or his niece might have tried to take out her ex-husband," Blaine replied. "I definitely doubt this was his first rodeo. Let's see what I can find out from Leroy Smith this afternoon."

ALONE WITH HIS thoughts as he drove to Chino State Prison, Blaine was ensnared by his worries. It had been over a week since Ainsley Brown was murdered, and he was no closer to an arrest than he had been on the night he met the young man's lifeless body. The insurance claims, Rodney's debt, and the previous attempt on Ainsley's life all pointed to Rodney's involvement, yet evidence-wise, he was batting zero. Hopefully, he would be able to get Leroy Smith to tell him something actionable.

THE CHINO PENITENTIARY, nestled in the Inland Empire region of Southern California, was an imposing beige structure surrounded by green fields and quiet country roads that were rare in that part of the state. It was a world unto itself, completely unfettered from the bustle of the city environs that encircled the compound.

Blaine parked and made his way inside, clearing the required checkpoints and signing in.

He knew it was risky to speak to Leroy Smith, given Rodney's affiliation with the FBI. While he liked Bedding and Defonso, he needed this visit to discover something he and Philips could use on Ainsley's case. He hated that he might upset the agents, but he hated the idea of Ainsley's murderer getting away more. He silently hoped Defonso and Bedding wouldn't catch too much hell. He either, for that matter.

Blaine's last stop before being able to meet with the inmate was to check in his firearm and place it in a locked cabinet. He was then admitted into the prison and escorted to an interview room to await Leroy Smith. Blaine wasn't sure what he expected to see upon meeting the man, perhaps a large, imposing figure that would cause a shiver of fear. He was anything but.

Leroy Smith was a small man, below average height, and skinny enough that he should be fearful of slipping through the shower drain should he get too close. His face was worn, and he was missing teeth.

Leaning heavily upon a cane, he had a distinct limp. A pouch was visible in the hip of his pants—a colostomy bag—courtesy the bullet he took during the LAX robbery.

Leroy sat across from Blaine while the guard who escorted Leroy stood just outside the door, assuring Blaine he would be nearby should there be a problem.

Blaine was fairly certain he could handle himself given the shape Leroy was in, but he did not voice this sentiment aloud.

"Hello Leroy, I'm Sergeant Detective Nick Blaine."

Leroy looked at Blaine's extended hand hovering in the air for a handshake which he refused by failing to extend his own. "What do you want?" Leroy asked tersely.

"How are you?" Blaine asked.

"Fine enough."

"How are things going?"

"I'm a cripple in prison, and I shit into a bag," came the answer. "How do you think I am?"

Blaine saw this wasn't going to be easy, but he pressed on. "The robbery that got you in here, what happened?"

"What robbery?"

"The one with Rodney Williams."

Leroy stared at him, defiant and yet somehow blank-faced.

"How long have you known Rodney, Leroy?" Blaine inquired.

Leroy continued to stare.

"Leroy, you've been in here for seven years. You said it yourself, you're a cripple who shits into a bag. Why not talk about Rodney with me? What can it hurt?"

Still, the man refused to answer.

"Have you ever wondered why the police were there so fast that day? How was it they were on the scene before you even got your hands on the money?" Blaine asked, hoping to at least stir the man's curiosity.

"I guess, yeah, I've wondered."

"Somebody set you up," Blaine explained. "Ever wonder who?"

Blaine watched as the countenance of Leroy's face changed. It went from bored indifference to a simmering rage.

"What prison did Rodney end up in?" Blaine asked, knowing driving home his point would rile the prisoner.

"I don't know. I never heard any more about him. I know Liam Edwards got sent up to Corcoran, but nobody told me where Rodney wound up. I figured maybe upstate somewhere."

"You didn't hear anything because he didn't go to prison." Blaine let the knowledge that he was betrayed slowly seep into Leroy's mind.

"He's still out on the streets, Leroy. He's a free man. How do you think that is? Why are you in here, and he's out there, free as a bird?"

Leroy started to pull himself up with his cane. He barely contained the rage mounting within.

"Have you heard from Rodney since you were put away? Has he come to see you? Has he written or called?"

Leroy was standing. The hand that rested on the cane was visibly shaking.

"Rodney Williams set you up, Leroy. He told the FBI what your plan was, and they informed the police. He then left you in here to rot on that bum leg and with that bag while he roams free. He's a paid informant for the FBI now, a job that you got him when you attempted to rob LAX. You've been in here serving time for his crime and you didn't have a clue what you sacrificed. He's getting a big payout from the Feds every month. A place to live on their dime, spending money, trips all over the place. And here you sit. You're decaying by the minute in this joint while Rodney's life is a laugh and teacakes. He's even murdered a kid. Yet, he still walks free. Help me put him away, Leroy. Tell me what you know about him. You've known him for years. You have to know something about him that we can use to stop him."

Blaine knew he was taking a huge risk telling Leroy who had put him in prison, but hoped it would lead to Leroy giving him information on Rodney. Instead, Leroy Smith leaned on his cane, turned, walked to the door, and banged on it so the guard would take him back to his cell.

Blaine left the prison with fingers crossed that his punt would work after Leroy had time to think about what had happened to him, thanks to Rodney Williams.

It didn't.

NOT LONG AFTER Blaine left the prison, Leroy made a phone call to Rodney Williams.

"Why hello, Leroy." Rodney was jovial in his reply to Leroy's voice over the phone.

"Rodney, why are you answering your home phone?"

"What do you mean?"

"Why aren't you in prison? Why isn't this number disconnected or somebody else answering?"

"You're assuming, my friend, that they caught me that day," Rodney countered. "And if they did, how do you know I haven't already done my time?"

"A detective was here to see me."

"Blaine?"

"Yeah. He told me an interesting story of how you set Liam Edwards and me up so you could get on as an informant with the FBI."

"Leroy Smith. You didn't believe him, did you? You know I ain't no snitch."

"Do I know that? I know I'm in prison, and you're answering your home phone."

"Now you listen to me, you piece of shit. Don't you go shooting your mouth off to Blaine or anyone else about anything you think your stupid ass might know. If I find out you did, that bag you crap in and that busted leg are going to be the least of your problems." Rodney was screaming and Leroy was regretting having made the call.

"Do you think I don't know people at Chino State Penitentiary? Do you think there aren't guards that would love to beat your ass? Who do you think has been keeping you from being dead this whole time you've been in there? You think just because I'm not in

Chino with you I'm not looking after you? Do you? You have a pretty good thing going on in there right now. Most one-legged criminals would be in a world of hurt in prison, but you manage to do okay. I think you might want that to stay that way, right?"

"Yeah, I guess so," Leroy replied.

"Okay then. Lose this number, and don't call me again."

The line went dead. Leroy stood looking at the receiver for several minutes before setting it down and hobbling away.

A week later, he was found dead in his cell. Not even his cellmate saw anything or anyone.

It took less than a week after Rodney's formal complaint to Bedding and Defonso regarding Sergeant Detective Blaine's visit to Chino for the FBI Director's complaint to reach the desk of the Los Angeles Chief of Police. The director demanded that Blaine be reprimanded at the least, fired at best. In the end, the matter hit the desk of Deputy Chief James Chisholm, who had Blaine escorted to his office.

Upon arrival, Blaine was unsure what would transpire. He braced himself for a spectacular ass-chewing and a formal write-up.

Chisholm, on the other hand, had other plans. "Blaine, have a seat," the deputy chief gestured to a plush leather sofa in his office and bade the detective to make himself comfortable. The chaperoning officer was dismissed with a wave of the deputy chief's hand. Chisholm then shut the door. Sitting behind his desk, he took out a bottle of Scotch and two glasses. "Drink?"

Blaine nodded, still somewhat wary and incredibly confused as to the cordiality he was being given.

Chisholm passed him a glass of whiskey and took a drink of his own as he lit a cigarette and relaxed. "So," he began, "what's this about the FBI getting their panties in a twist?"

18

Weeks passed, but Blaine and Phillips were no closer to catching Ainsley Brown's killer.

"What are we missing?" Phillips asked as he poured over the case information affixed to the corkboard in front of them.

"A witness willing to talk?" Blaine posited from his desk. Just then, the phone in front of him began to ring.

"Hello, Sergeant," the jovial voice at the other end greeted Blaine. "Have you changed your mind about giving me that letter so I can get things straightened out with the insurance company?"

"Rodney, you know I'm not going to do that. I can't help you. But maybe you can help yourself.

What have you been saying to the witnesses on this case?"

Rodney guffawed. "Sergeant Blaine, I would never impede an investigation. As an employee of the FBI, I know how important not meddling with an investigation is."

"Rodney, you're not an FBI agent. You're an informant. They pay you to rat out your friends."

"Now you listen here, Sergeant. If it weren't for me, the streets of Los Angeles would be crawling with drug dealers and murderers. I make the streets safer, and don't you forget it."

"Yeah, you make the streets safer, all right. Tell me, how many people have you and Randolph Barnes killed? Is Ainsley Brown safer? Leroy Smith?"

"I don't know what you're talking about," Rodney replied. "Oh, but I did talk to your friend, Conrad Knowles. Nice kid, He's scared to death something's going to happen to him, though I can't think of why that would be."

Blaine's eyes narrowed as the anger started to boil within him. "You leave that boy alone, Rodney. He's been through enough."

"Sergeant, I would never dream of hurting Conrad. He's like a son to me. In fact, he and I had a little chat a few weeks ago, and he told me all of Ainsley's homo friends in L.A. have been talking about me, saying I tried to have him killed in my garage before he was killed in the street."

"That's how I understood it, Rodney."

"That's a bald-faced lie, Sergeant. I wouldn't have hurt a hair on Ainsley's head. I loved that boy." Rodney started to make what might have been a whimper, but Blaine wasn't convinced it was anything but an act.

"What happened in your garage the night someone first tried to kill Ainsley?"

"Not a thing," Rodney answered quickly, "Ainsley and I were alone in my apartment. Ainsley was really agitated, and he used the phone a few times. I think he was fighting with one of his boyfriends. After a while, he got up and left without saying a word to me. He was like that, you know. He'd just leave with no explanation."

"Couldn't be because he was fighting to survive after being stabbed, was it?"

"Sergeant, I daresay if you would get your focus off of me, you might just figure out who the actual murderer is because, as I've said, until I'm blue in the face, it's not me."

"Rodney, my focus is on you because all the known facts seem to point to you being guilty as sin."

"Now look here, Sergeant Blaine, you need to get it out of your head that I did anything to Ainsley. The sooner you do, the better off you'll be."

"Rodney, are you threatening an officer of the law?"

"I wouldn't dare." Blaine could hear the smirk on the other end of the line.

"What do you know about Randolph Barnes?" Blaine asked, trying to move the conversation back to the questions he wanted answered.

There was a long pause before Rodney said in a low voice, "I wouldn't mess with him, Sergeant. He didn't do anything."

"Are you sure he didn't? I'm thinking maybe he's the one who shot at Ainsley and Conrad. I'm as sure of that as I'm sure you're the one who paid him to do it. I'm equally as sure you've been telling people not to talk to Phillips and me about this case."

"Sergeant, as I've said over and over, I know better than to impede an investigation," Rodney countered. "In fact, as a sign of good faith, I'll get anyone you want to come in and talk to you. How about that cross-dressing brother of ole' Phillips? Steven Oliver, I think her name is."

"Now you listen to me, Rodney, and you listen closely because I'm not going to repeat myself. Don't you go anywhere near Steven Oliver, or you'll find yourself on the wrong side of me. Do you understand? Now, either confess or get out of my way."

"I'll get out of the way," Rodney promised, "just as soon as I get that letter from you so I can get my money."

Before Blaine could reply, Rodney laughed and hung up, leaving Blaine to explain their conversation to his partner.

"What do you want to do next?" Phillips asked.

"I'm honestly not sure," Blaine answered with a heavy sigh. "Rodney Williams might not get the money, but he may just get away with murder."

19

November 1984

S ergeant Detective Blaine leaned back in his desk chair and closed his eyes as he sought just a few minutes of quiet and peace. The last few months had brought an onslaught of new cases that Blaine and Phillips were fervently working to close. As so often happened when he had a chance to reflect, Blaine began to ruminate on Conrad Knowles and his mother. He thought of them in their well-ordered home back in Chicago and those men who sat across the street each day, intimidating Conrad, eating away at him and any sense of security he may have known once upon a time.

On cue, the phone on Blaine's desk rang, fracturing his thoughts and turning his attention back to the present.

"Hello?" He answered a little tersely.

"Sergeant Blaine?"

"Yes, this is he."

"Sergeant, this is State Trooper Bart Blakely, down in Monroe, Louisiana." The man on the line had a thick Southern drawl.

The accent was comically thick to Blaine's ear, which drew his suspicions. There was no way this was a sincere call. Slowly, he leaned forward in his chair and craned his neck to gaze out around the room. Someone was pulling a prank, but who? "Okay," he replied, chuckling to himself as he eyed a young, cocky patrolman standing in a corner of the room, chatting on a phone.

"Oh, I got you," Blaine thought as he pretended not to see the rookie. He wondered who had put the kid up to it. No matter. He was on to them, and he began to plot his revenge.

"We have some information regarding a Rodney Williams that I want to discuss with you, Sergeant," the voice said.

"Oh, you do, do you?" Blaine remarked, impressed the young cop could keep up the ruse so long. It was no secret around Rampart Division that Blaine was somewhat intent, if not obsessed, with catching Ainsley's killer. In Blaine's book, that was Rodney Williams. He was a little surprised his coworkers would use the case for a joke, but maybe they were bored and having a little fun with him.

"Yes, sir," the voice replied. "I want to talk to you about Mr. Williams at length if you have a moment." The voice on the other end was beginning to sound confused if not a bit irritable, with Blaine's nonchalant responses.

"Well, if you need to talk at length, why don't you Louisiana boys come on out here to Los Angeles, and I'll give you my full attention and all the help you could need."

"Let me see what I can do, and I'll let you know." With that, the caller hung up.

Blaine, howling with laughter, peered at the young cop and signaled his approval with a large thumb up, to which the other officer smiled hesitantly and slowly returned the gesture.

Sitting back in his chair, Blaine was incredibly amused. He needed a break from the murder cases piling up on his desk and was pleased his fellow officers thought enough of him to pull such a gag.

As he regained focus and began working on the

case before him, his phone rang again. It was the same man.

"Sergeant, it's Bart Blakely again. We went ahead and got us some plane tickets. The undersheriff, Claude Ennis, and I are on American Airlines flight 208 out of Monroe Regional. We should be arriving at LAX around 9:30 PM your time. Do you think that maybe you could pick us up and give us a ride to the Sheraton Beverly Hills? That way, we can catch you up on our case, get the ball rolling, and catch ourselves a murderer."

Chagrinned and aware that Bart Blakely was anything but a joke, Blaine replied, "Uh, yes, that will be fine. We'll be there."

BART BLAKELY WAS a squarish man of average height with a happy, rotund face and tiny sparkling eyes. His companion, Undersheriff Ennis, on the other hand, was tall and gangly, built like a shovel handle with teeth to match.

As they walked to the parking lot, Blaine thought about the attempted heist at the airport, the one that made Rodney an FBI informant and put Leroy Smith in the hospital before ultimately ending up behind bars. Rodney had made a career out of deception and divulgence. Blaine wondered if Rodney had any remorse or if that was something of which he was even capable.

Blakely and Ennis marveled at the expanse of the Los Angeles area and were impressed by the largess of the freeway system. Neither man had been outside Louisiana, and Ennis had never been more than a few hours from Monroe.

"Are you y'all from here originally?" Ennis asked his hosts.

"I am," Phillips replied. "Blaine is from Podunkville, New York."

Blaine chuckled in response. "Phillips isn't too far off. It's actually a little town named Watertown, up near Syracuse."

"How did a small-town boy like you wind up here in L.A.?" Blakely asked.

"Well," Blaine explained, "When I turned eighteen, I was graduating high school and wasn't really sure what to do with myself. My father had passed, and my mom was single-handedly raising my brother and two sisters. I didn't want to be a burden on her when I could go out and get a job. So, I up and joined the Marines and wound up being stationed out here at Camp Pendleton. Next thing I knew, I was out of the service, married, and part of the LAPD."

"And the rest is history," Phillips added with a flourish.

"Enough about me. Are you guys hungry?" Blaine inquired.

"Famished," Ennis answered.

"How about some burgers?" Blaine suggested.

"That should suit us just fine," Blakely responded.

The men made their way to Tommy's, one of Blaine's favorite places to get a burger or a chili dog. They got to know one another over bites of beef and fries. Ennis was instantly smitten with the purveyor's milkshakes, taking one with him for the road before asking Blaine to bring him back for a roadie before he returned to Louisiana.

"Fun fact," Blaine said as they sat down to eat, "I investigated a murder here years ago."

"Really?" Ennis asked, "What happened?"

"There was this really short Puerto Rican guy in line for a burger. He was a security guard, and he just got off work. His wife picked him up, and they made a quick stop at Tommy's so he could jump out and grab a burger while she waited in the car.

'So, this guy was in line to order when this group

of drunks got in the line behind him and started mouthing off to him about his height."

"What did he do?" Ennis queried from the edge of his seat.

"Hang on, I'm telling you," Blaine responded with a laugh, "Okay, so the little guy got out of line and hopped back in the car parked at the curb. As his wife was driving away, the little guy took out the service revolver he used for work and fired some shots into the air, probably to show the drunks he was a tough guy. You know, short man syndrome or whatever. Tommy's security guard thought the shots were being fired directly at the customers in line. He took out his revolver and shot through the open window of the little guy's car as his wife was driving off. The car went about thirty feet before crashing into a cinder block wall. Turned out, the Tommy's guard shot the wife in the chest while she was peeling out and killed her."

"Talk about life being strange," Blakely quipped with a long low whistle.

"Yeah, that poor woman was just taking her husband for a quick burger, and she winds up dead. Who would think it?"

The men sat in silence for a few moments, each reflecting on the frailty of the lives they investigated.

Blaine finally changed the subject to the matter at hand. "So, tell us about Bobby Williams," he asked.

"Well," Blakely began. "It all started about two weeks ago when I got a call from Ennis here about a body on the side of the road just outside the City of Monroe."

"The Sheriff's department isn't equipped to handle murder investigations, so in the rare instances when one occurs, we call in the State Troopers to take the lead," Ennis explained.

"Right," Blakely concurred. "So, the victim in this case is a man named Bobby Williams, a resident of the area who had been staying at a local motel for the weekend. The poor guy was shot at close range, and his body was left on the side of the road.

"After we ran his record, we realized he had been picked up a few times on drug charges and were able to match his fingerprints to his record to confirm his identification. Next thing we knew, we got a phone call from a man at Equifax Insurance who told us the victim had an insurance policy, and the beneficiary was one..."

"Rodney Williams." Blaine cut in.

"Exactly. The brother of the dead man."

"And because we had flagged those policies, Equifax Insurance told you to give us a call."

"Right. And here we are. Before we left Louisiana, we interviewed Rodney Williams."

"Wait," Blaine interrupted, "Rodney is in Louisiana?"

"That's right. As far as we know, though, he's now back in Los Angeles. Slick fellow, that guy. We heard he covered Bobby's funeral."

"Let me guess, tons of flowers." Phillips chimed in.

"Yes," Ennis agreed.

"Actually," Blakely added, "We asked Rodney why he had gone overboard on the flowers, and he told us that he was the beneficiary on his brother's insurance policy, and it was his intention to spend every last dime of it giving Bobby a big send-off.

"He even told us that he was paying for the coffin and services, buying the plot, et cetera, and he used the rest of the insurance money on decorating the church. In all, he said he spent fifteen thousand dollars. Fifteen. Thousand. Dollars. On a funeral. Can you imagine?

"Naturally, we asked Rodney if there were any other policies out there on Bobby that listed him as the beneficiary. He assured it that there was only the one. It's funny. All I could think about the entire time he was talking to us was how he smiled like a Cheshire cat. He assured us several times that there was only the one policy, so it was no real surprise when we got phone calls from several insurance companies informing us that they had policies on Bobby Williams. Each one listed Rodney Williams as the sole beneficiary."

"I received a call myself," Blaine added, "Four months ago, following the death of Rodney's 'godson,' Ainsley Brown. We were informed there were nine other people with life insurance policies listing Rodney as the beneficiary. That's when we decided to flag the policies. Oh, that reminds me. You told me over the phone about an AmEx card that was used."

"Yes." Blakely cut in, "One of the things that stuck out in Bobby's case is that the motel in which he was staying and a rental car he had were both paid for with an American Express card issued to Rodney."

"I called the American Express Fraud line after I got off the phone with you," Blaine said.

"Which time? After the first call or the second?"

Confused as to why it mattered, Blaine answered, "The second."

"Well, I'm glad you didn't do any work before you were sure there really was a case," Blakely laughed, "Phillips filled us in about you thinking you were being pranked and all."

"Oh," Blaine said with a bit of a blush. "Yeah. I

kind of got a reputation about the Williams case out here. It's been a while since anything has happened on it. That day, I thought maybe one of the boys was taking his chance to have fun at my expense."

The men had a long laugh over Blaine's mistake before Blaine continued.

"Anyway, I called American Express to advise them that I believed Rodney's card was being used fraudulently down in Louisiana. We've contacted them and other credit card companies in the past, but they never did anything with the information we gave them. Usually, nothing comes of it. This time, though, a man called me back. A Jeffrey McDonald. He told me that based on the information he had been given, he was able to determine Rodney had filed nineteen separate applications for a credit card. Each application had different information, but it was Rodney. McDonald then informed me Rodney's card should never have been approved or issued. Because of the fraudulent applications, he wanted to file a criminal complaint listing Rodney as the suspect."

"What does that mean?" Ennis questioned.

"It means that due to it being a criminal complaint, we, the police, can ask questions regarding the use of any credit cards Mr. Williams might already have, including where or when he might have paid with them."

"Got it. And had he been using them?" Ennis was again on the edge of his seat with anticipation. He was a young man who was easily impressed. Blaine enthralled him.

"Yeah, Rodney used an AmEx card issued to him for a car rental and the Hillcrest Motel in Monroe, Louisiana. He also made a purchase at a sporting goods store in Jackson, Mississippi."

"Is that right?" Blakely asked as his mind started to whirr with the implications this information had for his case.

"We should call the boys back home and send someone over to Jackson," Ennis said to Blakely.

"Absolutely," Blakely retorted, "But it's nearly one o'clock in the morning back there, so there's no use in startling anyone and getting them outta bed. We'll give them a call first thing in the morning."

"That motel is known locally as a hotspot for drugs —dealing and using. We got all kinds of drug problems all over Louisiana right now," Ennis advised. "People are killing each other left and right over the stuff."

"For us, too," Phillips concurred.

Blakely nodded knowingly and continued. "We

asked Rodney why he was in Louisiana. He gave us some malarky about working for the FBI and that he was in Louisiana on some drug case for them."

"Oh, he does work for the FBI," Blaine replied. "As an informant."

"Any reason why Rodney would stay in a motel when he had his mom and other siblings living locally?" Phillips wondered aloud.

"Maybe he was using and selling drugs himself?" Ennis postured.

"Or maybe he didn't want anyone knowing he was there?" Blaine suggested.

20

From the moment they touched down in Louisiana, Blaine felt as though he was sweating through every orifice of his body, from his toenails to his eyeballs.

Blaine had not been prepared for the humidity when Blakely invited the Los Angeles detectives to Monroe to consult on the Bobby William's case. And then, there were the mosquitos.

"Hello, detectives," greeted a young trooper walking toward them from across the small airport. "I'm State Trooper Jay Kramer. Blakely asked me to come on over and take you folks over to the motel."

Kramer was a handsome young man. He had bright dark eyes that complimented his closely cut hair and richly-hued ebony skin. Tall and reed-thin,

Kramer's uniform seemed to have been tailor-made for him. Blaine thought Kramer could give Phillips a run for his money with the ladies if he were so inclined.

"How long have you lived in Monroe?" Blaine asked the youthful trooper as the car left the airport and approached the town.

"About eight years now," came the reply. "I'm originally from Kentucky, but I came down here to play ball at ULM and decided to stay after graduation."

Interested, Blaine leaned forward and asked, "What position did you play?"

"Receiver," came the answer, "You?"

"All of them."

"All of them?" Kramer asked, surprised. "Were you really talented?"

Amused, Blaine explained, "Well, I went to this very small, rural school. We played six-man football, and all the guys could receive a pass. So, we rotated positions."

"Ah, that makes much more sense," Kramer responded before asking Phillips if he had also played ball.

"I did," Phillips acknowledged, "But I was forced into early retirement."

"How early?" Kramer queried.

"Junior high."

"Injury?" asked Kramer.

"Yeah, my mom would've injured my dad if he let me keep playing. I was a scrawny kid who couldn't catch a glue-covered blimp two feet in front of me."

The car hummed along a few minutes more as the men told stories to the others' amusement before they came to a halt in the parking lot of a local motor inn. The outside of the place was freshly painted, and the entire motel appeared to be well-kept and much nicer than some of the lodges they had passed along the way.

"Here we are," Kramer announced.

"Are you sure this is the right place?" Blaine asked, peering out and noticing the large glass chandelier hanging in the lobby. "This seems much grander than the out-of-town lodgings we're accustomed to getting."

"When we heard big-shot detectives from Los Angeles were coming this way, the boss told his secretary to make sure she got you the best available."

Blaine and Phillips looked at each other and smiled at being called big shots.

"I guess he figured you guys are used to some pretty nice places out in California, and he didn't want you to think that Monroe couldn't compete," Kramer added as he helped the men with their luggage.

"Trooper Blakely asked me to tell you that he'll be here in the morning to pick you gentleman up and to make sure you're good and hungry when he arrives."

Blaine and Phillips agreed and shook Kramer's hand before checking in and getting their room assignment. The motel appeared new, and aspired to keep up with some of the better hotels in terms of amenities and appearance.

"I don't know about you," Blaine said to Phillips as he sprawled out on a bed in their room, "But I'm not used to being spoiled like this."

"Seriously," Phillips replied, "After that motel in Arcadia, I carry Raid and Lysol whenever I travel for work." Phillips reached into his bag and pulled out the cans of Raid and Lysol, which gave Blaine a chortling fit.

"I don't remember the last place being *that* bad," Blaine said when he had composed himself.

"Not that bad?" Phillips answered, feigning shock. "I shared my pillow with a family of roaches and used a large rat to warm my feet that night."

"Speaking of critters," Blaine laughed, "Let's go down to the restaurant and get dinner. I'm starving."

THE TWO MEN had a hearty meal of po' boy sandwiches and oysters before indulging in strong black coffee and beignets. They took a couple of Whiskey Slings back up to their room and sipped leisurely while listening to baseball on the TV. Both men quickly dozed off not long after resting on their beds, each slipping into happy, satiated sleep, the kind of sleep one enjoys after a night of overindulgence on good food.

THE NIGHT ROLLED on while the detectives rested until they were startled awake the next morning by Blakely pounding on the motel room door.

Phillips let the trooper into the room while Blaine explained that he and his partner would need a few moments to freshen up.

Blakely assured them they could take their time, reminding them that life ran a bit slower in the South than in California.

The detectives took lightning-fast showers. After alacritous primping, Blaine, Phillips, and Blakely grabbed a quick breakfast of coffee and grits before the trooper took the men to Hill Ridge Road on the outskirts of the city.

BLAKELY PULLED the car over and motioned for his passengers to join him outside.

"If you look down that way, you can just make out a few houses over there," the trooper advised as he pointed along an agrarian pathway made among the weeds and grasses that grew up alongside the road's path.

"One of those houses is where Rodney and Bobby Williams grew up. Their mother still lives there. Bobby's body was found when a guy had been walking down the road here and noticed a body lying in the grass next to the pavement. When forensics arrived, they took video and started collecting evidence. They found eleven spent .22 caliber Remington cartridge casings here where we are, and they spread across to about the middle of the road or so. There was a circular pattern of blood also in the middle of the road leading toward where Bobby was lying between the road and the little ditch over there.

"From what we can tell, on the night of the murder, Bobby Williams was lured out and was standing on the road when his murderer pulled out a .22 caliber rifle and started shooting. Bobby was hit and stumbled backward across the asphalt. In the meantime, the shots kept coming, each one blowing him toward the opposite side until he finally collapsed over there.

"The shooter left nothing to chance, either. Our head forensic scientist found that Bobby had been shot multiple times in his chest, both arms, and crotch."

Blaine was pained to think of the brutality with which Bobby Williams was murdered, especially the overkill of it all.

"When Ennis and I started looking on Bobby's person for identification, we found a receipt for a Federal Express money transfer from Rodney to Bobby a few days prior to the killing."

"I wonder if Rodney took the money back after Bobby was dead," Phillips conjectured.

"He might have," Blakely replied, "We didn't find any money at the scene, just the receipt and Bobby's driver's license."

Blakely looked up the way toward the Williams' home and sighed quietly.

"Ennis and I were the ones to go and tell Bobby's mother. A couple of her daughters and grandkids were there, which was good. The news wrecked the poor woman. She collapsed out of her chair and had to be helped to lie down before we left. As you can imagine, we weren't able to interview her that day. None of the other siblings was aware Rodney was in Louisiana at the time of the killing. They weren't surprised, though. I guess he's been telling them all he was working on some kind of super-secret drug case for the FBI, and it would be safer for them if he didn't make contact until the case was closed."

"Convenient," Blaine noted as he peered toward the homes in the distance.

"C'mon, let's go chat with the gun shop's purveyor over in Jackson. We called Mississippi State Police and asked them to have a preliminary chat with him. He was able to confirm the American Express card was in the name of Rodney Williams, but let's see if he can pick him out of a lineup." Blakely got back in the car and motioned for the other men to do so.

The trip over the state line to Mississippi was just under two hours, giving the men time to swap tales of crime and intrigue.

Blaine liked Blakely and thought he was the type of man who would make a good politician. He was honest, clever, and capable of speaking in an interesting and easy way. Years later, when Blaine heard that Blakely had been elected Sheriff, he wasn't surprised.

"Are you Tweed Lewis?" Blakely inquired as they entered the store.

"I am," the man confirmed in a thick accent.

"I'm State Trooper Blakely, and these gentlemen are Sergeant Detective Blaine and Detective Phillips out of Los Angeles."

Tweed Lewis nodded toward the cops and asked Blakely how he could be of service.

"I've brought a photo line-up I'd like you to peruse if you don't mind."

"I don't mind."

"There are a couple of pages, so take your time and let us know if you recognize anyone here."

"Well, this guy—here—in the left corner of page one, is the man who bought the .22 Remington Rifle. Rodney Williams."

"Are you sure?" Blakely inquired.

"Yep. And this man—here—a few pages over is the man that was with him."

"Did that man give his name? Did you hear his name while they were in your store?"

"No, but I'd recognize that face anywhere. His eyes are cold."

"Did the men say anything to you while they were in here?"

"No, but the Williams guy took off his glasses, and

I've never seen anyone that cross-eyed. His left eye was facing Dallas, and the right one, Fort Worth. That's a face you don't forget."

Phillips giggled a little in response.

Blaine shot him a look that advised him to behave.

Blakely thanked the shop owner for his time and left with Blaine and Phillips in tow.

"WE LUCKED out with that insurance information," Blakely stated as he got behind the steering wheel of the car. "And it was that call you told us about from American Express that put the murder weapon in the hands of Rodney and Randolph Barnes. That was our first big break in the case. The second was meeting Tommy White."

"Who is Tommy White?" Phillips asked.

"Our main witness."

21

Blaine and Phillips watched from an adjoining room in the State Trooper's station as Blakely spoke with Tommy White regarding what he had witnessed.

White was a scrawny man with a head that was substantial compared to his body. His teeth were long and stained from years of over-consuming coffee and nicotine. His eyes held an exhaustion known to men whose lives hadn't been as easy as they may have hoped. His hair was greasy, and his pale skin was acne-laden. White had an air of nervousness surrounding him. The kind that implied he had a chronic problem of being on the inferior end of a crummy situation.

"Mr. White, do you recognize any of the men in

these photos?" Blakely asked as he handed White a sheet of paper bearing the faces of six men.

"The one on the far right," Tommy explained, "That's Rodney Williams. The man on the bottom left is Randolph Barnes."

"I see," Blakely stated as he continued, "And how do you know Mr. Barnes and Mr. Williams?"

"Mr. Barnes, I only met a few weeks ago when they came to my house. I've known Rodney Williams for years. We went to school together. Rodney, his brothers, sisters, and my family. I've known the Williams family for years. Bobby stayed in contact even after I moved to Mississippi.

"Rodney made quite a few phone calls to you recently. Why is that?" Blakely asked. "Did you speak with him often?"

"I actually hadn't heard from Rodney in a long time before he called me a few weeks ago. Seriously, it had been at least ten years, and then he rang me up out of the blue. He said he was working for the FBI on a drug case to take down a "big one" and would be out this way. He asked if he could leave some stuff at my house. Then he called a few more times to make his plans to come here."

"And did he leave stuff at your house?"

"Yeah. He first came by the weekend before Bobby was killed. He brought that Barnes guy with him. That was the first time I met him. They'd been to a place in Jackson and bought a rifle, a .22, I think, and some ammo."

"Why did Rodney bring that .22 to your house?"

"He said he needed it just in case things got hairy with that drug bust he had been talking about non-stop. From the minute he got to my place, he chattered on and on about his work with the FBI and how this was gonna be the big one for him. Said he could take a break for a while afterward and relax."

"Did Rodney ever give you the name of the drug dealer he was talking about taking down?" Blakely asked.

"Nah, I wouldn't know him anyway, that was in Louisiana, and I don't use that shit," Tommy answered.

"Speaking of that, did Rodney say why he was buying a gun in Mississippi for a drug bust in Louisiana? And wasn't the FBI supplying him with a gun?" Blakely inched a tiny bit closer to Tommy as he invited the other man to reply.

"He said the FBI was gonna pay him back," Tommy responded. "Rodney said the FBI was real good about reimbursing him for things. He asked me where he could buy a gun cheap, and I told him about a sporting goods store here in Jackson that was pretty reasonable. I wouldn't be surprised if he used that gun for his FBI thing, then returned it and got his money back, but still gave the FBI the receipt. That's how Rodney operates.

"So, he left the .22, and then he came back about a week later and said the FBI bust was a go. He had intel where that drug deal was gonna be. Said his brother Bobby had set it up for him."

Blakely looked intrigued. "Did Bobby help Rodney out a lot?"

"Nah, I think this was the first time. Rodney wasn't gonna share his FBI money with Bobby for helping him. He just needed a dope fiend to make contacts for him. Bobby, he's had himself a problem for years. He tried to get sober once or twice, but it never lasted long.

"Anyway, so Rodney and that Barnes fella came back about a week after they'd been here the first time to pick up the rifle. I gave it to Barnes, and he sat down at my kitchen table and loaded it. He wasn't the most capable fella. He left a round of ammunition on the floor that he had dropped. I cleaned up after they left. It was the one I gave y'all when you first came by my place."

Blakely nodded in acknowledgment and asked White to go on.

"They left my place about four o'clock in the afternoon, and I didn't seem 'em again. But, after Rodney was arrested a few weeks ago, he gave me a call and asked me to lie about that .22, but I don't want no trouble, so I wasn't about to lie to y'all."

Blakely asked Tommy White if he had seen anything else. When he replied that he hadn't, Blakely saw the man out of the station and returned to his friends from Los Angeles. "Looks like we got some pretty decent info here, gentlemen," he said as he sat down.

"According to American Express, that card was used to pay for the guns, the plane tickets for Barnes and Williams both times they came in from Los Angeles to Mississippi, the motel where they were staying, a rental car, gas, and a few restaurants in Jackson and Monroe."

"He sure was keeping that card busy," Phillips commented.

"Yeah," Blaine agreed. "I wonder how much he owes on it."

Blakely nodded in agreement before adding, "That cartridge Tommy gave us was a match to those found at the scene of Bobby's murder, and fibers from a rented Beretta matched those found on Bobby's body. That, combined with the fueling up in Tallulah and the phone call Rodney made in Rayville, which is up the road, just before midnight, and I'd say we got ourselves a case. Thank God you all flagged those insurance policies."

"Yeah," Blaine answered. "Amen to that."

22

The July sun was searing as Rodney Williams came out of his house and headed for the black Chevy Cavalier in his driveway. As was his custom, he peered around the neighborhood to case his surroundings. He wanted to make sure nothing or anyone was out of place. As he surveilled the area, he noticed a silver Ford sedan parked up the road with what appeared to be two silhouettes. Rodney instinctively knew to whom those silhouettes belonged. With a smile and wave, he got into his car and left.

"Did he just wave at us?" Phillips asked Blaine.

"You know," Blaine responded, equally awed, "I think he did."

Phillips pulled away from the curb a few moments

after Rodney pulled away from his home and kept a tail on the Cavalier. Knowing they had been spotted and sure of Rodney's amusement with being followed, Phillips didn't try to stay as invisible as he otherwise would have.

As they wound their way through the neighborhood and onto the freeway, Rodney picked up speed until his car reached nearly 90 mph.

"I think he's giving chase," Phillips exclaimed, pressing his foot to the accelerator and matching Rodney's speed.

The two cars bobbed and weaved through traffic in a high-speed pursuit.

"Watch out for that VW," Blaine hollered as his partner took evasive action to avoid slamming into the slower vehicle.

"What is his plan?" Phillips shouted as he continued to hurtle down the freeway, dodging vehicles, and thankful there wasn't one of the traffic jams for which Los Angeles was famous.

Few of the cars on the road noticed the Cavalier's speed as Rodney and his vehicle continued to ascend upon them rapidly, with the police vehicle close behind.

Suddenly, Rodney crossed six lanes of traffic, nearly slamming into three other cars.

"He's getting off on Pico," Blaine called out.

Phillips glanced at the mirror before screeching across the freeway lanes.

Three cars behind Rodney, they watched as he slammed on his brakes and screeched into an Arco station.

With a lilt of the entire vehicle, the Cavalier stopped at a pump. Rodney emerged from the driver's seat as though he had been enjoying a slow and meandering day.

Pushing the brake pedal to the floor, Phillips brought the police vehicle into the same station at a side angle, narrowly missing an old Ford pickup vacating the premises. Smoke emanated from the tires as the police car jolted to a stop parallel to Rodney's. Blaine and Phillips jumped out with the momentum built throughout the chase.

As the cops bounded towards him, Rodney smiled slyly. "What brings you gentlemen out today?" he asked with sarcastic levity, "Did you come to finally give me that letter for the insurance company? Four months too late."

"I wish that were the case, Rodney," Blaine said as he and Phillips drew closer. "Turns out we received a fugitive warrant for you all the way from Louisiana.

Seems you're wanted for the murder of one Robert Williams. I think he's your brother."

"You don't say," Rodney replied, obviously relishing the moment.

"The FBI has already taken your friend Randolph Barnes into custody," Phillips explained as he withdrew his handcuffs from his waist. "Now it's your turn."

As Phillips put the cuffs on Rodney and walked him toward their car, Blaine gave him his Miranda warning. He then turned toward a nearby pump, where the gas station attendee watched closely. "Someone from the LAPD will be along for the Cavalier."

"Are we going straight to the station?" Rodney inquired innocently.

"We have to make a stop by your house first," Blaine replied.

"My house? Why?"

"Well, a search warrant was issued in conjunction with the arrest warrant. We need to execute it on behalf of the Louisiana State Trooper's office.

Rodney grew uncharacteristically quiet, and Blaine wondered if he was completing a mental inventory of what was in his house and calculating the risk of anything illegal being discovered. During the short drive to his home, he remained silent.

Blaine was suspicious as to why.

Upon their arrival back at the home, several other police units were there, waiting to enter for the calculated collection of Rodney's possessions. They wasted little time in hauling off guns and ammunition. They cataloged his clothes and shoes with precision.

Rodney remained stoic and silent as he watched his home rifled through. His face would not betray himself if he had anything illegal in his possession. He grinned slightly at a young officer advising Blaine they had found twenty-two credit cards in the desk. The grin evaporated quickly, and the steely-eyed stance he had previously presented returned.

"Hey Rodney," Phillips said as he walked into the living room with a file folder, "There are insurance policies in here for all your siblings and a couple of random guys. How did you get so many people to name you as their beneficiary?" Phillips handed the folder to Blaine.

Rodney remained silent.

The insurance policies in the folder revealed hundreds of thousands of dollars in potential payouts to Rodney Williams, including $240,000 for Alonzo Garcia.

"I'm glad Alonzo left town," Blaine thought, hoping the kid was safe from Rodney's reach. As he looked through the policies, he found a master sheet of names of those from whose deaths he would financially gain and speculated whether Rodney planned to work his way through the list. If that was the case, his brother James and his sister Ethel just got lucky. Their names were right after those of Ainsley Brown and Bobby Williams.

"Rodney?" Blaine questioned, "Who is Jorge Prado? His name is on this rejected insurance paperwork from J.C. Penney."

Rodney paused before replying as though he was getting his story straight before answering the detective's question. "He is my godson, Sergeant. Why? Would you like an introduction?"

"That's not necessary. I was just wondering who this kid was that had the good fortune to have his insurance policy denied before anything untoward happened to him."

Rodney stared forward and refused to engage, but Blaine could not let the moment slip past him, "Just how many godsons do you have, Rodney? What did you do to get all those mothers to trust you enough to make you godfather to their babies?"

Rodney could not help himself this time as he

retorted, "I'm just a trustworthy type of guy, Sergeant Blaine. All those mamas know that I'll take care of their little boys for them, especially when they're out here in California all on their own."

"Was Ainsley all on his own?" Blaine pointedly asked.

"Ainsley knew too many people to ever be on his own," Rodney answered, "In fact, he was so well known in certain circles. He may have made someone angry, and they killed him."

"Well played," Blaine thought to himself. To Rodney, he remarked, "Did he make you angry, Rodney? So angry you had to kill him? Maybe he was too popular, and you didn't like that he didn't need you anymore?"

"He would've always needed me, Sergeant. I was how his bills got paid."

"And how do your bills get paid, Rodney?"

"The FBI pays my bills."

"Is it the FBI, or are you, maybe, supplementing your income with insurance money? Maybe the insurance money of those kids you support who wind up dead, like Ainsley?"

"There wasn't anybody like Ainsley," Rodney remarked wistfully, "He was special."

"Special, but not too special to kill?" Blaine pointedly asked.

"Maybe he was killed because he was special, Detective. Did you ever think of that?"

"Did you kill him, Rodney?" Blaine interrogated.

Rodney smiled that Cheshire cat smile that made Blaine want to either choke or slap him. Maybe both. Then, slowly, Rodney leaned in closer to the cop and whispered, "I'll never tell."

23

As the search through Rodney's home continued, the detectives returned to Rampart Division. They tucked Williams into a secure interrogation room to await the arrival of the authorities from Louisiana.

Sitting at his desk, Blaine thought about Ainsley and wished he had enough evidence to have charges brought up on Rodney Williams for the kid's murder.

"You're thinking about the kid again, aren't you?" Phillips inquired, stirring Blaine from his reverie.

"I am. I know Rodney was behind it. I know in my gut he had Ainsley Brown killed. And Barnes pulled that trigger."

"I agree," Phillips acceded, "Unfortunately, feelings

don't equate to court filings. And we both know the system doesn't always work. Sometimes it fails, and real justice is an accidental by-product."

"Yeah," Blaine acknowledged, "I don't think we'll ever have what we need to put the weapon in Barnes' hands. Not as long as they keep poor Conrad Knowles too terrified to testify. Another case of justice denied." Blaine sat back and sighed deeply.

"Let's go get something to eat," Phillips proposed.

"Now that is something I can get behind." Blaine stood and gathered his keys.

"You know what I need," Phillips said as he held the door for his partner.

"A drink?" Blaine guessed.

"That too, but what I really want is a hot dog from Pink's."

"I think we have time for that. Blakely and Ennis won't be here for a couple more hours."

On their way out of the precinct, Steven Oliver stopped the detectives in the lobby.

"John." He said, nodding to his brother.

"Steven."

"I'll meet you in the car," Blaine advised his partner as he made his way out of the conversation.

"What can I do for you, Steven?" John asked.

"I heard that Rodney Williams has been arrested."

"He has."

"Good, the streets are safer with that prick off them. I just wanted to come in and hear it for myself."

"Steven," John started with a lilting voice, "I want to apologize."

"What for?"

"Everything. For our past, our parents, and being a jerk to you all these years. You didn't deserve that. It's taken me a long time to get out of my own way, but Ainsley's case has meant something to me. He was your friend, and I couldn't get justice for you."

"Well, he's going to prison, isn't he? I know it's not ideal and isn't for Ainsley, but he is going away."

"Yeah, but still."

"Sure, it would be nice. But I guess there was something to it all."

"What do you mean?" John asked.

"Well, without Ainsley, we wouldn't have crossed paths after all these years."

"True."

"And you wouldn't be here eating crow."

John started to laugh. "Yeah, I guess. Is it too late for us to start over?"

"It is. Way too much water has passed under that bridge. But we can go forward from here."

"I would like that," John replied, holding out his arms to hug his brother.

"I'm not hugging you," Steven said, punching his brother in the arm. "Have we ever hugged? Like in all of our lives, have we ever hugged?"

"We had to have, right?" John answered while rubbing the spot on his arm where he had been slugged before pounding his brother's arm in return. "Wanna have dinner tomorrow night and catch up?"

"Are you buying?" Steven inquired as he and John moved towards the door.

"Yeah, I guess."

"Then yeah, you can take me somewhere nice, and I'm getting the lobster."

Phillips laughed.

Steven turned and hugged him before saying, "I'll meet you tomorrow at seven PM at Judy's Cafe."

"Okay."

Steven strode away, and Phillips joined Blaine in the car.

WHILE THEY DROVE through Central L.A., Blaine thought about the city. Los Angeles was a beast, made up of concrete and rebar, skyscrapers, and throngs of people pushing their way through life, trying to make it day to day. "Rodney suggested that someone killed Ainsley because he was popular," Blaine disclosed.

"Rodney would say that. That man is as evil as cotton candy."

Blaine turned to look at his partner for a second before having a quick chortle and asking, "What the heck does that mean?"

"You know," Phillips explained, "He's evil, but he's also soft and sticky, like cotton candy."

Unable to hold in a burst of laughter, Blaine let it out.

The partners roared with laughter for several moments, feeling a wave of relief wash over them. The moment of levity was exactly what they needed. The day had been long and their time with Rodney Williams was interminable. They continued to banter and joke around as they ate, briefly letting go of the crime and heartbreak that surrounded them in their vocation.

When they arrived back at Rampart Division, Blakely and Ennis were there waiting to greet them, ecstatic that Rodney was in custody. Following the usual salutations, Blakely cajoled Blaine into sitting with Rodney one last time before they extradited him back to the South.

"He has a rapport with you," Blakely pointed out.

"Yeah," Phillips concurred, "Like Tom and Jerry."

"I think if he's going to admit to anything, it's going to be to you," Blakely rationalized.

"Okay," Blaine acquiesced. "I'll give it a try."

Blakely, Phillips, and Ennis watched the video feed as Blaine sat across from Rodney at the little table in the interrogation room. Blakely held his breath, hoping Blaine would be able to turn the screw enough that Rodney would give them something verbal with which to work. Not that their case needed it, but an admission would be icing on the cake.

"Rodney, we've known each other for a few months now, right?" Blaine asked.

Rodney nodded in agreement.

"This is a serious matter you've gotten yourself into. Before we talk about it, I want to advise you of your rights. If you want to talk with me, fine. If not, then that is entirely up to you. You don't have to say anything. Okay?"

"Jesus Christ," Rodney muttered. He was seemingly astonished at his situation and irritated that he was in it at all.

"Rodney, let's play by the rules, you understand? You have the right to remain silent. If you give up that right, anything you say can and will be used by you in

a court of law. You have the right to speak to an
attorney and have an attorney present during ques-
tioning. If you so desire and cannot afford an attorney,
one will be appointed to you without charge. Do you
understand?"

"Uh-huh."

"Now, do you want to talk to me, Rodney?"

"I don't know."

"Listen, Rodney, this involves a murder in
Louisiana. Was someone you know murdered there?"

"My brother," Rodney replied.

"Your brother was murdered?"

"Right." Rodney began to loosen up, leaned back in
his chair, and became amenable to talking again.

"Okay. Is that it? Why would they implicate you in
the murder of your own brother?"

"That's what I would like to know, Sergeant. "When
did this happen?" Rodney asked.

"When did what happen? Blaine replied.

"When did they send you a warrant for my arrest?"

"This morning. They called us this morning and
faxed a copy of the arrest warrant."

"I can't believe this," Rodney mumbled.

"Rodney, that's what I'm getting at. Do you want to
talk about this? Do you want to talk to me? "

"What do I have to talk to you about, Sergeant Blaine?" Rodney started to laugh. It was a deep, guttural laugh from a man who knew his life had taken a bad turn, and he had nothing left to do but find humor in the circumstances.

"Christ, Rodney. It was your brother. Your brother was murdered. Gunned down in the street less than a mile from your mother's house."

"I'm at a loss here. Why would I murder my brother?" Rodney stopped laughing but smirked at Blaine while they verbally sparred.

"And you were there. If your brother was murdered, you must be a suspect. You know what I mean? I can't talk to you unless you want to talk to me, and you need to state for the record that you want to talk to me before I can talk to you. You either want to talk to me, or you don't. And if you don't, that's fine, you can go to booking. We have the arrest warrant. The next step is booking you."

"Jesus Christ. I can't believe they would do this." Rodney said quietly.

"You were in Louisiana recently, weren't you?"

"Well, I went back there for the funeral, right? I went to the funeral for Bobby and all that. But how could they? I had a run-in with two deputies while I was back there. They swore up and down they were going to nail me and everything. We had been talking to the Sheriff's guy around there, Enos or something."

"Ennis?" Blaine suggested.

"Yeah, Ennis has been asking questions back there. He talked to my sisters and my mom. But I know his boss, the Sheriff. Sheriff Buchanan. He's a good friend of mine and everything."

"Okay," Blaine replied.

"They said my brother, Bobby, was shot over ten times back in April. I think it was the 29th or the 30th. So, I went to the funeral along with the rest of the family."

"That must have been a tragedy."

"Well, it was." Rodney leaned forward across the table. "What is today? Monday?"

Blaine nodded in affirmation.

"I can't believe this," Rodney repeated. "I can't believe this."

"Why, Rodney? That's what I'm getting at. Why can't you believe it? Is there something you want to tell me? Do you want to talk to me about something?"

Rodney began to laugh again, somewhat maniacally. "Why Blaine?" He laughed, "What do I have to talk to you about?"

"Christ, Rodney, it was your brother."

"I'm still at a loss here. Why would I kill my brother? It's funny, isn't it? They think I killed my brother. On Friday, that Friday back in April.... he had a heart attack and a stroke. All those years of using drugs were catching up to him, so I went back there to check on him. I'd been staying on top of it. Golly, I can't believe this is happening."

"Well, I don't know. What *is* happening?" Blaine questioned. "When was the last time you saw your brother?"

Rodney thought a moment, "Last year? I think it was last year or maybe the year before. I don't really remember."

"Look, we know each other. That's why I wanted to admonish you. I wanted to be straight with you. I don't want you to think I'm jacking you around."

"I know the FBI," Rodney interjected, "And I know they've been staying on top of everything."

"Sure, I would assume they know of your whereabouts." Blaine agreed. "You're from where, Monroe, Louisiana?"

"Right."

"When was the last time you were back there?"

"For the funeral. That was the last time I was back there. That was the only time I was back there. I don't go back there often."

"But," Blaine cut in. "Didn't you go to Grambling College?"

"Yeah, I went to Grambling. I've got a Bachelor's from Grambling."

"Do you still go back there for ballgames?"

"Yep, every year."

"And when you go back there for the games, how do you usually get there?"

"I fly into Jackson."

"So, you fly into Jackson, Mississippi, and drive to Grambling, Louisiana?"

"That's right."

"That's on Interstate 20?"

"Yes."

"Doesn't the route from Jackson to Grambling go right through Monroe - where your family lives? Where Bobby was living?"

"Who was it that called you? Was it Ennis?"

"No," Blaine returned.

"Was it the Sheriff?"

Blaine pretended to think a moment before saying, "Um, I think it was Buckley. No, Blakely. Trooper Blakely. That's the one."

"Blakely? With the state troopers?" Rodney squirmed a little on the metal chair and appeared to look uncomfortable.

"Why wouldn't the state go through the FBI?"

"I don't know. Why would they point at you for the murder? We... we aren't talking about insurance policies again, are we?"

Blaine felt a sense of triumph at bringing the conversation around to the insurance policies, especially given Rodney's propensity for getting people in his life to take out such policies.

"Well," Rodney responded, "I'm the overseer of my family's insurance, Nick."

"How much did you have on Bobby?"

"Bob had some four hundred thousand dollars in insurance. My sisters have that much, too, because they took it out really young. I have six hundred thousand on me."

"Oh yeah?" Blaine countered, "Who's your beneficiary? Is it me?"

Rodney laughed hard for several moments before replying, "No, my son, my sister, and my mother are the beneficiaries."

"You have a son, Rodney?"

"He lives in Belize."

"Really?" Blaine had heard rumors that Rodney had a mysterious son who lived abroad. Conrad told him nobody had met the boy, not even Coretta or Ainsley.

"Yeah," Rodney replied. "He's Belizan."

"Where is Belize?" Nick inquired, "South America?"

"Central," Rodney corrected him. "They speak Spanish there."

"I see. Why does he live down there?" Blaine asked.

"That's where his family is."

"All those boys we picked up at your house earlier today, those "sons," they're not blood-related to you?"

"You picked up my boys?" Rodney was incredulous and found it difficult to contain his anger. "What did you do with them?"

"We brought them in. We asked them some questions. Then, we let them go." Blaine explained.

"What else did they take from my house?"

"Um... records, phone records, things like that."

Rodney's eyes narrowed. "What telephone records?"

"For your home telephone," Blaine explained, knowing he was being coy. "Your checking accounts and credit card statements, things like that. I'm not going to look at them. Louisiana will pick it all up, do what they want, and go from there. That search warrant was in conjunction with the warrant for your arrest."

"My files were locked. How did they unlock them?"

"I don't know. Your files were taken into custody."

"Did they take the whole cabinet?"

"Not the whole cabinet, just the files."

Rodney began to squirm in his seat. His breathing grew shallower.

Blaine noted the beads of sweat on William's face and knew he was on to something.

"Did they take all the files?" Rodney inquired.

"Yep, all of them. They didn't leave a scrap of paper behind," Blaine assured him.

"All the files that were in there?"

"Yes."

"So, they broke into the filing cabinet?"

"It would seem so, yes."

Flustered, Rodney said, "You didn't know where the key was. It was on my key ring."

"Which one, the key ring with the keys to your car?"

"Yes," Rodney affirmed.

"Oh shit, we gave those back to you."

"What?" Rodney was confused.

"Your key ring."

"No, I don't have my car keys."

"Well, they were with you when you came in here. They were brought in with you, I think."

"I thought you would give the keys to David, the kid I asked you to give them to when we were at the house."

"Well, we intended to bring David in here, too. A couple of the boys hanging out at your house had warrants. We're trying to decide whether or not to book them."

"Who had warrants?" Rodney asked, his voice rising.

"Let's see," Blaine sat back in his chair and put his hand to his face. "There was David Agulard."

Rodney cut in. "Hector. Hector didn't have any warrants, did he?"

"Well, yes, he had one," Blaine conceded. "But we've given him the benefit of the doubt and told him to get his ass on down the road. He gave us a bullshit story, but I thought you had been sitting in here long enough and didn't want to delay any further while we tried to get him sorted out. So, we told him to get his ass down to the courthouse tomorrow and take care of the warrant, and we let him go."

"What about David?"

"Agulard?"

"Yeah, David," Rodney questioned. "He had warrants?"

"He has two warrants."

"He took care of those," Rodney clarified.

"Oh, well, they're still in the system. It may well be that the court hasn't cleared them."

"And Mario?" Rodney inquired.

"Mario, yeah, we'll release him."

"But you're going to hold on to David?"

"Yeah, on the warrant."

"Come on, Nick," Rodney howled. "Those boys are going through enough now as it is."

"I can imagine," Blaine commiserated, "I bet you getting arrested is real tough on them. I sure was surprised when I got the warrant to arrest you."

"Why did you get the warrant?" Rodney asked somewhat belligerently. "Aren't you stationed here at Rampart? I live up in the northeast."

"Yeah, I didn't know you were over on Clayton Drive. We had to do some digging to hunt you down. Last we knew, you were over on Angora."

"Well, he had my address."

"Who did?"

"That state trooper, Blakely, he knew where I was living. He knew I wasn't in your area no more."

"You know, Blakely might be how we got your address. I'm not sure how they knew to call me, but they did."

"Mmm hmm." Rodney rolled his eyes as he looked at Blaine in disbelief. "Do you have their warrant?"

"Yep."

"Can I see it?"

"I don't have it on me, but it was very straightforward. It says you're being charged with one count of murder."

"Just because I'm the beneficiary on Bobby's life insurance?"

"Well, I don't know. Was it one or two policies?"

"Five."

"There were five policies on your brother, and you were the beneficiary of all five?"

"Yeah," Rodney conceded.

"I don't know what in the world they have on you. I just wanted to be upfront and advise you of your rights before those boys from Louisiana get here to take you away."

"Did you guys take the FBI records, too?" Rodney asked.

"Did we what? Oh, the FBI records. Yes. Now, wait a minute. We must have. We took all of the records from your place."

"I can't believe this shit." Rodney stared down at the table and mumbled to himself.

"They needed to look through everything, I

suppose. They took your payment statements, credit cards, and credit card applications. There were a lot of those I heard. At least twenty."

"This is bullshit."

Rodney stared at Blaine for a moment, but he was no longer defiant. Instead, he appeared to be searching for his next logical move.

"This is unbelievable." He muttered, buying time to think. "And you have all of my client's records as well?"

"You'll have to straighten that stuff out with Louisiana's authorities about your clients. Who are these clients?"

"Did you tell Hector what was happening, Blaine?"

"Hector? Hmmm.... Hector. I did talk to Hector." Blaine was enjoying himself immensely. "Oh, yes, we told him what you are in custody for and that you would definitely be remaining with us."

"How did Hector get home?"

"Those boys are all young and have good legs. They were ready to take off and walk home. They didn't seem to want to stick around here."

"Also, Nick, could I have something to eat? We were fasting at church and I haven't had anything to eat since six o'clock last night."

"Okay, hold on."

"I've got the money for a sandwich or something," Rodney offered.

"You want a sandwich and maybe a soda?"

"Yeah."

"And you've got a dollar?" Blaine asked jokingly.

"Yes, and I'm starving. Can they also add a bag of chips or something?"

"What the hell do you think I'm running here? A catering service?"

Rodney laughed, and Blaine left the room, chuckling. He then entered the room where Phillips and the others had been sitting, listening to the conversation.

"I called out for a sandwich," Phillips advised.

"Thank you," Blaine said with a nod.

"You're doing well in there," Blakely stood up and slapped Blaine on the back. "Maybe once he's had a bite, you can get him to talk some more."

The door opened, and a young woman handed Blaine a plate of food and a drink.

"Round two," Blaine called out as he left and re-entered the interrogation room.

"Mr. Rodney H. Williams, here you go, the finest dining Rampart has to offer."

"Thanks, Nick."

As Rodney ate, Blaine continued to talk.

"Well, I never thought we'd be sitting here so soon.

It's only been a few months since Ainsley's murder. I thought maybe we would be sitting here in an interrogation room together at some point, but I figured it would be further down the road. I haven't seen you since that day we had lunch. You look good."

"What else do you have to do now? Book me?"

"Well," Blaine started, "As far as I'm concerned, when you get through enjoying that meal there, yeah, we'll take you down and book you in and then get you started on your way back to Louisiana."

"When do I go?"

"Whenever the authorities from down South are ready to take you."

"They can come now if they want to 'cause I'm ready for their shit. Did you say they have all of my bank statements?" Rodney asked.

"Yep."

"They don't have my actual phone conversations, do they?"

"Now, that I don't know. You're being clever with me. You know, they have the bills and things like that. Maybe they have the records of the conversations."

"Hmm. Okay." Rodney looked uneasy again.

Just then, the door opened a crack, and the young woman who had brought the sandwich advised Blaine that he was wanted elsewhere.

"You behave yourself, Rodney, and good luck to you. I have to go to see what they want."

"Hey Nick," Rodney said, relaxed again now that Blaine was leaving.

"Yeah?"

"Can I get another sandwich? Your catering company does good work."

EPILOGUE

September 1985

"How did you get in here?" Blaine asked Phillips as he exited the baggage claim area of the airport and found his partner sitting quietly reading the newspaper.

"They had a special. Let one cop fly, and their partner gets to wait for him, twiddling his thumbs for free. What happened in Louisiana?"

"Rodney Williams has been found guilty of murder by a jury of his peers."

"Good, he needs the vacation. I hear prison is lovely this time of year."

"Rodney was sure surprised when the jury foreperson read the word guilty."

"I'll bet. In his mind, he was only guilty of loving too much and caring too deeply. How was your testimony?"

"Fun," Blaine answered as they walked through the airport. "Rodney's lawyer, this Paul Childs guy was determined to paint me as corrupt and out to get his client. The DA even told me Childs was planning on sending a letter to the chief outlining what an unscrupulous bastard I am."

"How dare he accuse you of being unscrupulous. I can't wait to hear what the chief makes of that," Phillips laughed.

"Neither can I."

"The good news is, while you were in Louisiana, we got a couple of new cases."

"Anything good?" Blaine asked with interest.

"Well, how do you feel about a fortuneteller to the stars? She was found face down on her crystal ball."

"Hmm..." Blaine pondered aloud, "I wonder if she saw it coming."

Made in United States
Cleveland, OH
10 January 2025

13289356R20129